Claire Lorrimer began her v
She was encouraged and influen
Robins, author and founder member of the Romantic Novelists' Association. On leaving school, Lorrimer worked as sub editor on a women's magazine. During the Second World War, serving as a WAAF officer, she began to write light romantic fiction for various women's journals. Her literary work later included some sixty light romantic novels. She subsequently turned to historical fiction. Meticulously researched, these novels on an epic scale feature the lives of passionate and striking heroines set against a strongly drawn historical background of many different eras. They often highlight the situation of women. She lives in rural Kent and is currently busy writing her latest historical novel.

BY THE SAME AUTHOR
ALL PUBLISHED BY HOUSE OF STRATUS

Chantal
The Chatelaine
Fool's Curtain
Frost in the Sun
Last Year's Nightingale
Mavreen
Ortolans
Relentless Storm
The Shadow Falls
The Silver Link
The Spinning Wheel
Tamarisk
A Voice in the Dark
The Wilderling

CLAIRE
LORRIMER

The Secret of Quarry House

This edition published in 2001 by House of Stratus, an imprint of House of Stratus Ltd, Thirsk Industrial Park, York Road, Thirsk, North Yorkshire, YO7 3BX, UK.
Also at: House of Stratus Inc., 2 Neptune Road, Poughkeepsie, NY 12601, USA.

www.houseofstratus.com

Typeset, printed and bound by House of Stratus.

A catalogue record for this book is available from the British Library and the Library of Congress.

ISBN 0-7551-0337-8

Chapter One

'Joanne, tonight I've met the man I want to marry!'

I'd been waiting all evening for my flatmate to return from the theatre to make my announcement and I was so excited, the words came out in a near squeak.

Jo, my best friend since our school days, flopped into the nearest armchair and kicking off her high-heeled shoes, stared at me with appropriate astonishment.

'But I thought...'

'Yes, I know...' I broke in. 'Tim was coming round.'

Tim was my most recent boyfriend whom I liked but certainly did not love and although I'd written to him he refused to believe I wanted to end the relationship unless I told him so to his face. Joanne had advised me to let Tim come round to the flat and get it over with. It hadn't been easy and I hated having to hurt him. He was convinced that there was another man in my life; and I had been trying to convince him otherwise when the doorbell rang.

'And there he was...the man I want to marry, Jo!' I told her breathlessly. 'Just the way it happens in books – love at first sight!'

Jo grinned.

'Well, I suppose it had to happen eventually,' she said, 'although I'd about given up hope.'

I threw a cushion at her.

'I'm hardly on the shelf at twenty-four!' I protested, laughing.

'Okay! But all the same, Tim was far from the first to get the cold shoulder. You invariably find something wrong with all your boyfriends...'

I sat down beside her and felt a rush of affection for this plump motherly friend of mine. In many ways, she really had 'mothered' me although she was only three years older than I. I had lost both my parents when I was eleven and my only living relatives were an elderly uncle and his equally elderly wife. Already retired, my uncle had been a bank manager and was one of my father's trustees. Neither he nor his wife were unkind to me; they did their 'duty', overseeing my education, health, upbringing. But they had not really wanted a young girl foisted upon them and were relieved when Jo's family invited me to spend my holidays with them. Jo was a senior at the private boarding school my uncle sent me to and had obviously felt sorry for me. As I grew up, we became friends and when I left school, we decided to share a flat together in London. It was Jo who found me a job at the Berman School of Languages after I had got my degree at college.

'You're looking for a father figure!' she told me more than once when I'd explained that most boys of my own age seemed far too young; that I was only at ease with older people. It was true that I had adored my father and perhaps I was trying to find someone I could love and respect as much as I had him. Now, miraculously, he'd appeared on the doorstep!

'Are you or are you not going to tell me what happened!' Jo said with pretended exasperation. 'Who is this miracle man?'

I drew a deep breath, excitement still holding me in its grip.

'His name is Campbell Rivers. He is thirtyish and a widower. His home is in Yorkshire but he has a flat in London where he works. He's tall, dark and terribly handsome – distinguished looking...'

I broke off, remembering that first sight of Campbell when I opened the door. I'd noticed his eyes – dark, compelling; and the way he dressed – elegant but not stuffy! We'd stared at one another for one long minute and then Tim, whom I'd momentarily forgotten, came up behind me.

'So there is someone else!' he said, jumping to a wild conclusion that could not have been further from the truth at that moment. 'You could at least have admitted it, Kate...'

And he'd stormed out, brushing shoulders with the stranger who was looking from one to the other of us in complete bewilderment. I know it was unkind when Tim was so obviously hurt as well as angry, but I couldn't help smiling at his dramatic exit as he rushed down the stairs and out of my life.

'At that time,' I explained to Joanne, 'I thought Campbell had come to see *you*, so I invited him in. 'This is Flat 2a, isn't it?' he asked, at which point I realised he wasn't a friend of yours. He wanted those people in 2a which I explained was, oddly enough, on the next landing.'

'Well, go on, Kate,' Jo said as I paused.

I spun out my story, happy to relive it as I did so. Campbell Rivers had followed me into the flat and I'd closed the door before we had discovered the mistake. He started to apologise but I explained that his surprise visit had turned out to be fortuitous since it had the effect of ridding me of Tim's persistent presence. Relieved he hadn't embarrassed me after all he'd smiled.

It seemed the most natural thing in the world for us both to sit down and start talking. Cam introduced himself and explained that he did not know the tenant in Flat 2a but was delivering the bottle of champagne for a friend, as our building was on his way home.

By the time he left, we'd consumed the champagne between us – and I was in love.

I did not then know Cam's exact age. His face, long and thin, already a little lined, struck me as sensitive and beautiful. His voice was deep and soft and perfectly modulated. I loved the way he laughed and the intense direct way he stared at me when he was talking – as if what I said really mattered to him.

Jo put an arm round my shoulders and hugged me.

'So that's why you're on cloud nine!' she said. 'And when are you seeing this paragon of all the virtues again?'

'We're lunching tomorrow!' I said. 'Can I borrow your red skirt, Jo? I want Cam to see me looking a bit more sophisticated than I did tonight.' I glanced down at my faded jeans and old T-shirt and wondered what on earth someone like Campbell Rivers could have found attractive about me. But he must have liked me to invite me out to lunch.

'Don't be such a goof!' Joanne said. 'You underestimate yourself, Kate. You'd look fantastic in an old potato sack. Lucky old you with that size ten figure and those fabulous green eyes. And sometimes, you can even sound intelligent!'

I threw another cushion at her and then we made tea and turned in since both of us had jobs to go to in the morning and it was growing late.

Our lunch next day – at a smart French restaurant where Cam was obviously well-known to the headwaiter – was an extension of the previous evening. I did something I had never done before and played hookey so that I could spend the afternoon with him. We were still discovering each other at dinner time and it was two o'clock in the morning before he took me back to the flat and kissed me goodnight.

The more I learned, the deeper I fell in love. But a week later, my radiant happiness had given way to a deep depression. I was afraid – not of what was to happen later, of anything positive – but of the negative fact that while he seemed as eager for my company as I was for his, Cam showed not the least sign of falling in love with me. I was terrified he would leave London for his home in Yorkshire before I had any chance to implant myself sufficiently deeply in his mind and heart. I was afraid that once away from me, he would instantly forget all about me.

Joanne thought I was crazy, not just because I'd fallen so quickly in love with a total stranger, but because I doubted that Cam was in love with me.

'My dear girl, of course he's crazy about you. I never saw a man more obviously smitten. But the whole affair is ridiculous; he must be twice your age!'

'What if he is!' I said, annoyed and as touchy as anyone suffering the pangs and glories of first love. 'I don't care how old he is. I love him!'

I was terrified he'd walk out of my life as mysteriously as he'd walked into it. I knew he was rich and with his looks, I felt sure he must have a dozen or more beautiful, sophisticated women chasing him.

I found that Cam had a great many other people in his life. I was shaken to discover that he was, at the comparatively young age of thirty-eight, already twice a widower. He had first married at twenty-two, a woman several years older than himself, who had a small daughter. His wife had died four years later in tragic circumstances he did not describe and left him with a stepdaughter of six. Partly for the child's sake, since his business interests often took him to Europe, Cam quickly remarried his stepdaughter's nanny. In the subsequent five years they had three little girls, now aged eight, ten, and eleven. His stepdaughter was eighteen. His second wife had died three years ago.

Until I met Cam, I imagined that I had had a sadder life than most people, losing the parents I had loved when I was still a child. Fate had seemed very cruel. Now Cam's past life seemed even sadder.

He told me he had never really loved his second wife. He was fond of her, and she was good to him and to the children. He had not been unhappy. She had given him three little girls whom he adored, and between them and the building up of his business abroad, his life had been full enough. Or so he had thought until he met me. Then, he told me, he realised for the first time how empty it had been of the most necessary ingredient of all – love! He was, he told me, head over heels in love with me. I was delirious with happiness. We behaved like every pair of lovers, walking, talking, holding hands beneath the dinner table of our favourite restaurant, telephoning each other for hour-long calls if we were unable to meet each day. I wrote love poems to him. He sent me flowers. When he went home for the Easter holidays, I was so restless and miserable that I nearly drove poor Joanne mad.

But Cam, too, was suffering from our separation, and when he returned to London, on our first night out together, he finally asked me to marry him.

I was so happy, excited, and relieved that I burst into tears. I cried all the way to the restaurant, Cam hugging me and looking quite desperate because he had actually believed I was going to refuse him! When I calmed down, he told me he had been trying for months to pluck up courage to ask me to marry him – as if courage were necessary! I would have said yes that first weekend. But he had quite naturally imagined that a girl of my age would shy away from the thought of four stepdaughters, one only six years younger than myself. Moreover his home was in a remote part of Yorkshire, with little or no social life, and marriage to him would automatically mean I would have to give up the career which I had described to him in such enthusiastic terms.

My darling Cam – it showed how little he really knew or understood me that he could doubt I would give up twenty careers to be with him. I would have taken on twenty stepchildren, too! Besides, I had always thought that one day I would like a large family. I loved children and, being an only child, a large, happy family represented security and the companionship I had lacked.

Joanne's reactions to the news that Cam and I were going to get married as soon as possible were strange and, to me, perturbing. She accepted that we were both genuinely in love, and yet she showed no enthusiasm of any kind when I talked of our marriage. She agreed that Cam was nice, kind, generous, as well as charming, attractive and rich. She agreed that we seemed ideally suited: accepted that the age difference didn't seem to matter much to either of us and that I'd always preferred older men anyway.

I really had to put pressure on her to admit the real reasons for her misgivings. When she told me what was in her mind, I felt an enormous surge of relief.

'Call me superstitious if you like, Kate,' she said, kneeling in front of the electric fire drying her beautiful long chestnut hair, 'but I just don't like it – both Cam's former wives died in tragic accidents. Aren't you scared out of your wits that you may be number three?'

I laughed. But Joanne refused to laugh with me.

'But third time is lucky!' I said, throwing a hairbrush at her. 'You are not seriously trying to make me see my beloved Cam as a Bluebeard, are you?'

She turned her head slowly and looked up at me, her eyes so serious that the laughter faded from mine. She ignored my last frivolous remark. 'I still think you ought to go up to Yorkshire – see the house, meet the children, look around, find out more about everything – before you get married. Honestly, darling, it's crazy not to do so.'

'But why?' I asked, shrugging my shoulders. I couldn't take Joanne's remarks seriously, but it was so seldom she got maternal with me, that I was forced to listen.

'I don't know.' Joanne said with a flat honesty that impressed me more than wild surmises might have done. 'Say I'm silly if you like. I just have a feeling – here!' She put her hand to her head. Then suddenly she gave a nervous laugh, as if she were ashamed of what she was about to say... Joanne who always spoke first and thought afterwards. 'I'm the seventh child of a seventh child, and Irish to boot. Call it a premonition, if you like.'

My laugh came out a little louder than I had intended. 'Are you claiming second sight?' I asked sarcastically. To my surprise, Joanne did not answer. Usually she was sharp and quick with a comeback when I teased her. I relied a lot on Joanne's intelligence. She was a highly successful career woman, independent, resourceful and down-to-earth. She had a wonderful sense of humour, and was not superstitious.

'I think you must have been reading *Rebecca!*' I said, turning away with a strange feeling of apprehension. The book was a favourite of mine, and I knew Joanne had read it, too. In a way, my circumstances and those of the heroine were not dissimilar, both of us marrying older men, widowers, whose wives had died tragically.

I found myself thinking about it later that night in bed, but then I knew I was being silly. Cam had not been in love with his second wife, Jennifer. Unlike Rebecca, she wasn't in the least attractive, judging by the photo Cam had shown me, although she had a nice, friendly face – the sort of woman who knitted and baked and turned the sheets sides to middle – ordinary, domesticated, plump, and kindly.

Cam didn't tell me much about his first wife. On our honeymoon in Majorca, he said he preferred not to remember her. She had married him for his money, and he had been deeply scarred by discovering, a few months after their wedding, that she had no love to give him. Money was the only thing in the world that mattered to her. Nevertheless, it had been a terrible shock when she had slipped on a craggy path on one of the mountains behind the house and fallen to her death on the rocks below. He had been in Europe at the time and had flown home for the inquest. A kindly Yorkshire woman had taken the little girl, Muriel, into her home, and Cam's main preoccupation at the time had been to see that the child did not suffer too greatly from her mother's death.

He had tried to give the little girl as much love and attention as he could, but she had a strange, reserved nature which barred any of the usual physical demonstrations of affection. She didn't care to be hugged or cuddled, and after a while he found it easier to leave Muriel in the care of the woman with whom she seemed perfectly content. He might have left this domestic in charge for some time but for the fact that, after a year, the woman said she could no longer continue with the fostering as she had a growing family of her own on whom she wished to concentrate. That was when Cam engaged a nanny – Jennifer, who subsequently became his second wife. The big old house in the Yorkshire hills, closed down after the accident, was reopened, and within a year the first of his daughters was born – a happy, laughing baby they christened Sandra. Debbie and Lillian followed soon afterwards and Quarry House was filled with the pleasant, homely paraphernalia of prams and nappies and ironing airing on the nursery fender, toys scattered on the green lawns in summer and over the big Persian rugs in the drawing room in winter.

Cam told me that those early years were happy ones in a calm, soothing way. Jennifer was an excellent housewife and mother, and he adored his baby girls. The only fly in the ointment was Muriel who, understandably enough, was showing signs of jealousy of the new arrivals. Cam himself did not have to deal much with the girl's silent oppressive moods since he was frequently away on business and had a service flat in London where he stayed when necessary. But he had known that Jennifer found the going tough. A less placid nature than hers might well have wilted under the thankless task of trying to bring a smile to Muriel's face.

Cam thought that boarding school might be the solution as soon as she was old enough, but Jennifer pleaded for the child, pointing out that she might feel they were trying to get her out of the way, thereby increasing her jealousy. Muriel herself begged and pleaded to remain at home. Jennifer was giving her adequate lessons and, she told him, she was perfectly happy at home. She liked to run wild on the moors and in the hills and did not need the companionship of children her own age. She promised Cam that she would be no further trouble to Jennifer – indeed, she would help more with the little ones if he would permit her to stay at home.

'So naturally she did not go away!' Cam told me. 'I've sometimes wondered if I did right to let her remain at home. The little ones were too young for her to play with, and she led a solitary life. When Jennifer died I felt guilty that the poor child should have to live through a second tragic death. For several weeks she shut herself up in her room and spoke to no one. It was a terrible shock for her even though Jennifer was not her mother. I've no doubt it brought back memories of her own mother's death. This time I insisted that she should get right away from home into a good boarding school. I found a housekeeper to look after the babies, and as soon as they were old enough, they, too, went to boarding school. Muriel, of course, has now left school, but the others are at home for the holidays. So you see, my love, you are going to have your hands full.'

I suppose of the four children, my sympathies lay most with the solitary Muriel, odd-man-out in the family. Although I knew Cam had shown her only kindness, she was not his child. She must have felt this deeply when his own little girls arrived on the scene. I resolved, if it were at all possible, to make a special attempt to befriend her. With only six years difference in our ages, it might be possible for me to break down the barrier she had obviously built around herself, and become her friend. I was not likely to forget how, only a few years ago, Joanne had made herself my friend when I was alone in the world. Now I would do my bit for Cam's stepdaughter. As for his children, I had no doubt I would love them since they were a part of him and I loved him to the point of insanity. The mental affinity between us had been complemented by the perfection of our physical relationship. He was, to me, the perfect lover. He did not have to tell me what I felt in every pore of my being – that he loved me as passionately and fully as I loved him.

Cam spoke during our honeymoon of the children we would one day have. I suggested teasingly that his family was quite big enough already. But Cam reminded me he had no son.

'I'd like at least one boy,' he told me. 'But not yet, my darling. First I want to give you time to get used to your ready-made family. Then, when you can take them in your stride, we'll think about having a child of our own.'

I wanted whatever Cam wanted. At the same time, I knew that if he wanted that son now, I would instantly become pregnant. I was feeling, for the first time in my life, the primitive urge to carry the child of the man I loved so desperately. I forgot my interrupted life's work – my career. Nothing mattered to me now but Cam and his happiness. My own lay simply in being with him. As long as I could be near him I was content. I could listen to his deep, resonant voice for hours on end and when he turned his head and smiled at me – not the worried smile I had noticed when we first met, but one of total joy – I wanted nothing more from life. I determined that he would never be sad again.

'Tell me more about Quarry House!' I asked him on our honeymoon. I lay curled against his long, hard back, my arms clasped around his slim waist, my face burrowed in the curve of his shoulder. I loved to lie like this with the whole of my body touching his. When we lay in the reverse way with Cam pressed against my back, my front felt lonely despite the warmth of his hands over my breasts. 'Funny girl!' he'd say but I think he understood my desire to be both physically and mentally near. That's why he never refused to answer my endless questions.

Quarry House had been bought by Cam's father – a wealthy Lancashire cotton merchant. Cam had been brought up in Yorkshire amid beautiful lakes and moors, riding his pony, fishing in the rivers, leading the kind of life all young boys desired. Although his father was a self-made man, he was determined to have his boy educated as well as possible and he was sent to a good public school and on to university. Unfortunately the idyll of the boy's childhood was interrupted by the death of Cam's father from pneumonia. His mother lived long enough to attend Cam's graduation from Cambridge and then she, too, died.

Cam was shrewd enough to see that the rapidly dwindling fortune his father had amassed would be better invested out of cotton. He started an export business in London which soon began to pay dividends. Quarry House remained shuttered and empty until Cam's marriage. Remembering his own childhood, he thought that his stepdaughter would enjoy the same happy, carefree childhood he had enjoyed there. He persuaded his new wife to open up the house and restore it to some of its former comfort and beauty.

'Neither of my parents was artistic,' Cam told me. 'Father was practical and called in experts when he bought Quarry House. It was badly in need of repair, but Father was determined to live there because it was a unique building and the land was valuable. So he paid a big price and an even bigger one for the restoration. That's why Quarry House is now as lovely as it was three hundred years ago.'

Later, I was to discover for myself that Cam's house was a Jacobean mansion of considerable beauty, but now I sat leaning against his knee, listening with breathless interest to all that he described. It was obvious that he loved the place.

'Incidentally,' Cam told me, 'Quarry House has taken its name from an abandoned quarry half a mile away.'

Both Cam and I were fond of history, so I was interested in all he had to tell me. His home had been built in the reign of James I, and during that period the influence of Flanders had been at work even in Yorkshire. Quarry House was a gem of that period, magnificently panelled in rich old oak. The dining-hall ceiling was vaulted.

'I think you'll like the plastering in the drawing room, too,' Cam added in the eager voice he used when he was describing his home. 'I can't wait to show it all to you, darling.'

'Nor I, to see it,' I said.

'Not only is it beautiful indoors, but the moors are splendid,' he went on. 'We can see them from the top of the house. We also have a lake at the end of our grounds. Beyond that is the valley; then the land rises again up into the moorland. It's pretty isolated, except for the odd shepherd and farmer. We rarely meet people, and the tourists usually visit Yorkshire to see the better-known places such as Wuthering Heights – the Brontë parsonage. Our property is even wilder, more sequestered than most. Thank goodness our nearest neighbour is three miles away.'

I smiled and sighed with contentment. I could picture it all. It sounded marvellous, and I didn't mind how many miles away the neighbours were, nor how lonely Quarry House would be. I was enjoying an entirely new emotion – possessiveness about another human being. I wanted Cam all to myself. The fewer people I had to share him with, the happier I'd be. I knew he'd frequently have to be away on business; he had already warned me that he might not always be able to take me with him. But he promised, if it were ever to be for more than a week, he'd arrange that I went too, provided I could amuse myself while he attended his dreary conferences.

'At least I'm well enough off financially to be able to buy you a ticket to anywhere in the world whenever you want it,' Cam said reassuringly. 'And unless you want it otherwise, I shall keep Mrs Meadows on as housekeeper so that you are not always tied down by the children. Believe me, dearest, I want you with me whenever it's humanly possible. Now that I've found you, I don't intend to have you out of sight if I can help it.'

So Cam could be possessive, too!

I was very, very happy.

'You look like the proverbial cat who's licked the cream!' Joanne told me as we stopped off for drinks at the flat on our return from Majorca. We were going up to Quarry House that afternoon by car, and I had one or two suitcases I wished to pick up.

'I have everything in the world I want,' I told Joanne. For the next few minutes I bored her with rhapsodies about Cam and how wonderful married life was.

'Wait till you get to Yorkshire!' Joanne said darkly. 'That's when this "great wonderful love" will have to meet the test!'

I laughed. I was looking forward to meeting my ready-made family. The snapshot Cam had shown me of his three little girls could not have been more appealing; their serious little faces and big wistful eyes seemed to call to me to come as quickly as I could and bring some gaiety into their lives. Moreover, they all three strongly resembled Cam. They had his large, wide-apart eyes and high, intelligent forehead. The truth was, Cam had evoked so much love in me that I felt I had enough and to spare for all his family.

I had no regrets at leaving London. Although I had many acquaintances, there was no one with the exception of Joanne to whom I was deeply attached. I had said good-bye to my business colleagues before my marriage. The past had become completely meaningless to me and I wanted nothing but Cam and the future.

Why then, I asked myself as we drove up to Quarry House in the summer sunshine, should I suddenly have this strange feeling of apprehension? I stole a glance at Cam's face. He looked happy, relaxed and I knew was excited at the thought of seeing his children again and introducing them to me. There was nothing in him to evoke the uneasiness within me; nothing about the big grey house with the glorious trees casting dappled shadows on the lawns to explain my sudden shiver of fear.

'I'm just tired!' I thought, remembering that Cam and I had slept little the night before, for our love-making was still new and wonderful enough to make sleep seem a terrible waste of time.

Cam braked gently in front of the heavy carved door and turned to look at me.

'Happy, sweetheart?' he asked in that deep attractive voice I so loved to hear.

'Wonderfully, darling!' I answered.

But it was a lie.

Chapter Two

As we entered Cam's house – my home now, too – we were surrounded by brown and white King Charles spaniels jumping up at Cam. Cam, watching my face, laughed.

'I forgot to tell you about them. You don't mind them, darling?'

'No, of course not!' I said. I'd never had a dog of my own as a child, and in a London flat with a full-time job, it didn't seem fair to have pets.

There was a sudden rush on the stairs and three little girls in blue jeans and yellow T-shirts descended in a heap upon their father. I stood watching as he tenderly hugged each one in turn. For a moment or two he quite forgot my existence as he listened attentively to their excited welcome. I felt curiously alone – outside the family circle. Then Cam turned and put his arm around me.

'This is your new mother!' he said simply. 'You may call her Kate.'

Three pairs of eyes stared into mine with a mixture of shyness, curiosity, and speculation. I sensed their uncertainty of me, a stranger who had come into their lives through no choice of their own, and resolved there and then that they should never regret their father's choice of a new mother for them.

'This is Sandra...Debbie...Lillian.'

As in their photograph, they were all very alike; slender, attractive little girls, with only the youngest, Lillian, retaining the unformed look of babyhood. They said their polite greetings. I noticed that Sandra stuttered. I wondered if she were the most highly-strung of the trio. Lillian took a tentative step towards me and touched my new scarlet jacket – it was what Joanne called my 'honeymoon special'.

'It's pretty!' she said with a shy smile. 'You're pretty, too!' I was touched by the compliment. In fact, I had never considered myself in the least beautiful. My nose was too Grecian for my liking, my mouth too big, and my eyes too small. But I think when I fell in love with Cam, I did in a funny way almost become beautiful. Cam thought so, and that was enough for me. Still, I was strangely pleased to hear his little daughter say the same thing.

I bent down and ruffled her hair, thinking she probably did not want to be kissed by a total stranger, but she suddenly flung her arms around my neck and hugged me.

'I'm glad you've come,' she whispered. 'I'm glad.' It was almost as if she were arguing the point. Had she imagined I might turn out to be an ogre?

With Lillian still clinging to my hand, Sandra and Debbie to Cam's, we went into the drawing-room. I was struck at once by its formal beauty. It looked as so many lovely rooms looked when photographed by the glossy magazines – just a little too neat, the flowers arranged just a little too perfectly, like a stage scene. But not like a room that is lived in.

It was L-shaped, the parquet flooring polished to a rich gold and spread with two magnificent rugs. The pale rose-pink and gold incomparably soft colours led me to suppose they were French Aubusson carpets. I realised they were priceless and was surprised and rather amused that the dogs were allowed to rush around this room, rolling on the floor and rubbing their long silky ears against the two sofas upholstered in magnificent striped cream and pink satin.

On the shining surface of a grand piano stood a number of photographs, mostly of the children; but half-hidden behind them was a studio portrait of a woman with a kind gentle face, I later learned that she was Jennifer, Cam's second wife.

From one of the three tall windows opening into the garden I could see a marble nymph and flower beds everywhere. The purple and blue of delphiniums, the splendid tiger lilies, the beds of pink and scarlet peonies, and the long borders of spice carnations bore witness to a good gardener. Indoors or out, the colours were pink and blue and gold – exquisitely blended, like the fine Minton china on a silver tray which was laid out for tea on a walnut table between the centre windows. In the high Jacobean fireplace stood a wrought-iron basket, ready laid for a fire. Above the carved mantelpiece hung a magnificent gilt-framed painting of the three little girls whose faces were soon to become so familiar to me. But the portrait that caught and held my attention was at the far end of the room – the painting of a girl with long blonde hair, so fair that it was almost white. This was Muriel, Cam's step-daughter. I had imagined her to be dark. Those huge, thickly lashed green eyes were just as Cam had described them to me. And now Muriel, with a friendly smile, was advancing across the room carrying a large tea tray. I saw Cam smile at her.

'We're being formal today, aren't we? Usually we have tea in the garden or in the nursery. This tea party must be in your honour, Kate darling.'

I did not comment. For some unknown reason, I shivered. Cam, always sensitive to my needs, bent down and put a match to the fire.

'The sun's gone in. You're cold,' he said.

The dry wood caught at once and crackled cheerfully as the strong draught from the long high chimney sucked the small flames up into a blaze.

Little Lillian came and squeezed my hand. 'I like fires,' she said softly. 'They comfort!'

I had no time to consider what she meant. Everybody was talking at once and the tea party was about to begin.

With a strange, gliding grace, Muriel held out her hand to me.

'Welcome to Quarry House,' she said. 'Do sit down and be comfortable. I nearly lit the fire earlier but I wasn't quite sure if' – she paused looking at me apologetically – 'if Kate felt the cold or not. Is it all right for me to call you Kate? Father wrote to us of you and always mentioned you by your first name.'

'Yes, of course!' I said smiling. I was favourably impressed by Muriel's pleasant welcome and graceful manners. She had a Victorian quality about her. The pale blue linen skirt she wore was fashionably short and the matching sweater plain enough not to be dated. Yet she didn't look out of place in this Old World setting.

With complete self-assurance, she handed out the teacups. The younger children were quiet now and seemed to take their cue from Muriel who wanted, I thought, to show me that she wasn't a child, as they were, and could play hostess as well as any adult. She seemed older than her eighteen years, but then that was not surprising considering the life she had had. I felt a stirring of sympathy for her. I, too, had had to grow up too fast, was always mature for my years. I found myself hoping very much that Muriel did not in any way resent my arrival at Quarry House. Obviously in the absence of a mother, she had taken on the role. I resolved to be tactful in taking over my obligations to Cam's family.

While Cam chatted with his younger daughters, Muriel sat at my elbow, quietly drinking tea. She was perfectly composed, elegant, and calm.

'I hope my coming here will make life easier for you, Muriel,' I said sincerely. 'You must find it very quiet and lonely at times.'

She looked at me with just the faintest trace of a frown. Her skin was fantastically white, I thought, without a trace of tan. Browned as I was by the Majorcan sun, I remarked the difference and said, 'You'll be able to get out and about more now I am here, won't you?'

'But I do go out whenever I wish,' she replied. 'Mrs Meadows does all the housekeeping. I am quite free to come and go as I please.'

I had not intended to sound pitying. I realised then that this girl was immensely proud. I must be more careful in the way I spoke to her. Despite what she said, I felt sure her life was far from normal. Most girls of her age did not live at home these days. They had jobs, flats shared with girlfriends, careers. Impulsively I put my hand on Muriel's. Her skin was cool and satiny to touch.

'We're really so close in age, I hope we will be friends.' I said. 'I'm going to need your help with the little girls, and it will make a big difference to me having you there to tell me their likes and dislikes and their routine.'

For a moment she did not reply but withdrew her hand as she reached across to take my empty cup from me. Then she said, 'You won't have much trouble with Sandra – she's easily managed. And Lillian, of course, is too young to be really difficult. Debbie is more of a problem. She is very strong-willed. She's also very jealous. She won't like Father paying you more attention than he pays her.'

I looked across at the child, sitting cross-legged on the floor, her back leaning against Cam's knees. One of his hands was lying gently on top of her head. She looked perfectly at peace – not in the least rebellious or difficult. But then she had Cam's full attention. I must take care, I reminded myself, not to be possessive with Cam in front of the child.

I suppose that was the moment when I first fully realised that Cam wasn't just my husband and lover, but a father. I don't think it was exactly jealousy I felt but a sudden isolation – as if I were outside this magic circle. Sandra was leaning over the back of Cam's chair, a hand on his shoulder. Lillian was curled up beside him on the sofa. They made a charming picture, but Muriel and I were outside it.

Then Cam turned his head, his eyes searching for mine, and smiled at me. It was a smile full of warmth and intimacy; the same expression of peace and happiness I had seen there so often after we had made love. I knew he was happy, and my feeling of anxiety ceased to have any importance.

'I think we'll go up to our room and unpack,' he said, disentangling himself from the children, his eyes still on me. I knew then that he wanted me to himself.

'Come along, children,' Muriel said, and there was a sharpness in her voice I hadn't heard before. 'I expect Kate is tired. You'd better go and tidy up the nursery.'

Her authority seemed as absolute as that of any governess. The girls voiced no protests and followed Muriel obediently out of the room. Cam looked at me smilingly. 'Well, what do you think of them all, darling?' he asked as we made our way upstairs.

'They are all most attractive children,' I told him sincerely. 'And Muriel is beautiful. You never told me.'

'Didn't I?' Cam asked. He seemed surprised. Then he grinned at me. 'I expect I've been far too busy telling you how beautiful you are!'

He held my hand tightly as we walked up one of the two curved staircases leading to the landing. They were quite beautiful, a rich mahogany with barley-sugar balustrades. The walls were panelled like the rest of the house, and the landing formed a gallery hung with paintings of hunting scenes which Cam told me had been bought in Brussels. The various bedroom doors opened on to the landing, as did the door to the nursery.

Cam stopped and opened one of the doors, leading me into the bedroom which was to be ours.

He put his arms around me and kissed me.

'Happy, darling?'

I clung to him, dazed by all I had seen, unable to say more than 'wonderful' and 'beautiful'.

I was overawed by the size of our bedroom – at least thirty feet long with three windows overlooking the garden across the parkland to the fringe of the moors beyond. The bed was a four-poster with massive twisted mahogany pillars, hung with deep red velvet curtains drawn back by tasselled satin ropes.

Downstairs everything had been pink and gold. Up here it was crimson – the draperies, and the velvet brocade bedspread all in the same rich colour.

Modern cupboards had been built all along one side of the room, but there were several old-fashioned chairs and a chaise-longue upholstered in crimson satin. A beautiful walnut spinet had been converted into a dressing table. Snow-white curtains looped across the windows, and a magnificent crystal chandelier gave the room a bright touch. Cam turned the light on and flooded the room with a golden glow. Instantly it looked warm and inviting. I admired the adjoining bathroom – modern and shining. Cam switched on two big electric fires in the main room.

'Oh, darling, it's wonderful!' I told Cam. 'I love our room. I love it all, and we're going to love each other in here so much, so much!' I felt suffocated with happiness.

He pulled me against him and kissed me – a long, deep kiss which turned my insides to water.

'I love you,' I whispered when he at last freed my lips.

'And I love you more than anything else in the whole world,' Cam whispered back.

Later, as we lay side by side in the big double bed, Cam confessed that he had never known total happiness until now. 'I suppose there have been many times in my life when I believed I was happy,' he said, his chin, a little rough now and in need of a shave, pressed against my bare shoulder. 'But deep, deep down inside me, I knew there was something missing. I know now what it was – love. I have never loved anyone but you, Kate. I can still scarcely believe that we're married – that you're my wife – here in my home beside me. Hardest of all to believe is that you love me.'

I couldn't speak. How, I wondered, could anyone not love Cam.

He murmured sleepily, 'I wish I had not wasted so much of my life without you, darling, that I did not feel so guilty marrying you. You deserve someone young and unmarked by life. I've no right to land you with four stepdaughters, one nearly as old as you are.'

Now I found my voice. I told him indignantly that I'd never been in the least attracted to immature young boys, that I was thrilled to have four ready-made children, and that I fully intended to make the family even larger as soon as we'd all settled down and his children had accepted me and learned to trust me. As for Muriel, I was going to make a special friend of her and she of me. She would be a great help in managing the younger children.

Cam leant on one elbow and looked down at me, his face suddenly thoughtful. 'I sometimes wonder if Muriel has too much control over the children,' he said. 'It may not be good for them to be so totally dominated by her.' He sighed, relaxing once more by my side. 'On the other hand, Mrs Meadows has no control at all, and I suppose it would be quite wrong to let them run wild. I expect Muriel is right to be so firm with them. I've been lucky to have her here to manage the children, though at times I've felt guilty in allowing her to act as a kind of governess to them. But she always assures me she's perfectly happy staying at home. She paints, you know. I had the room over the stables done up as a studio for her, and she spends most of her free time in there.'

'*Does* she?' This was news to me but I don't think I was really surprised. Artistic talent fitted with Muriel's solitary nature and the strange inner strength I imagined lay within that cool exterior.

'Abstract stuff!' Cam said sighing. 'I don't understand it.'

I said smilingly, 'Well, so long as she is happy, darling, we needn't worry about her.'

'All the same, I do worry a bit,' Cam said. 'She has this rather unsavoury boyfriend, Logan Winter. She sees a great deal of him. Personally, I find him an arrogant, lazy, insolent, self-opinionated weakling!'

'Them's mighty strong words, pardner!' I commented. I was surprised to hear so much condemnation from Cam who was usually so tolerant.

But Cam was not in the mood to discuss Logan. 'Even the thought of him makes me furious,' he said. 'I know I'm probably being unreasonable and I promise I'll tell you all about him at another time. But not now, darling. I'm too happy lying here beside you. Besides, I'm sure I haven't told you lately that I love you?'

'Not for at least ten minutes!' I lifted one of his hands and held it against my face. I wondered sleepily if there ever came a point at which one ceased to fall deeper and deeper in love. The more I was with Cam, the more deeply I loved him. Each time I thought 'I'll never love him more than I do at this minute,' a time would come soon afterward when I knew that I did.

I tried to explain this to him. 'Surely it must come to a halt somewhere?'

'I don't see why there should be any limit to love,' Cam answered. 'It's a growing living thing, darling. I think if it didn't grow deeper, it would start to recede. Oh, Kate, my love, just suppose you should one day wake up and realise that you loved me less.'

'Impossible!' I exclaimed with total conviction.

'Until death do us part!' At least, I think that was what he said, but he was holding me so fiercely against him, that I couldn't be sure.

Chapter Three

We had two weeks together at Quarry House before Cam had to return to London on business. I was to have gone with him, but little Lillian suddenly developed a high temperature, and at the last moment I felt that I should make the sacrifice and remain at home. Already Quarry House was beginning to feel like home, especially Cam's and my private suite.

We had our big sunny bedroom looking down on the lovely green parkland, a small sitting room and luxurious big bathroom all to ourselves. Its position, at the end of the long passage, gave us privacy from the rest of the household; the children's rooms, Mrs Meadow's room and the spare room were sufficiently remote to make it seem as if Cam and I were quite alone in the house.

It was typical of Cam's sensitivity to have realised that much as I wanted to be a mother to his children and make our home happy for them, too, I still needed a place where I could be nothing but his wife; where I could have him all to myself and feel like any other new bride. Here I could forget that he was a widower and that two other women had lived here with him. With the children it was different.

There were times when one or other of them mentioned their mother. On every occasion Muriel angrily hushed them, as if anxious I should not be pained by a past in which I had no share. Once I had to check her for forbidding them to mention their mother's name again because it might upset me.

'It's not true, Muriel, although I appreciate that you were only trying to be tactful. I think the children should talk of their mother, and you of your mother, too, if you wish.'

Muriel's face set in stiff, taut lines. She had been so kind and helpful I was sorry to have to overrule her but as I endeavoured to explain to her, it was a question of principle. Children shouldn't have to bottle up their feelings.

'Perhaps you don't fully understand!' Muriel argued coldly. 'Jennifer drowned. The children know it. When her body was discovered, she was bloated almost beyond recognition. I don't think it is a very pleasant subject or one they should be encouraged to talk about.'

I was shocked at Muriel's bluntness and suddenly uncertain of myself. I had indeed forgotten the tragic aspect of Jennifer's death, and indeed had never known any of the details. I'd felt that Cam would have told me if he'd wanted me to know, and since he never spoke of it, I never questioned him. I was thoroughly unnerved by Muriel's cold-blooded description. But after a moment's reflection, I thought I could understand it. She, alone of the four children, was old enough at the time of Jennifer's death to be most deeply affected by it. It is often easier to speak of something shocking in a detached way, as if one were reading an account in the paper. Maybe she was right, and it was best if the younger children forgot their mother. I was going to ask Cam's advice, but that evening Lillian developed a fever, and my concern for her put all other thoughts out of my mind.

Although he hated going back to London without me, I could see that Cam was touched by my decision to stay with Lillian. He knew I preferred to be with him, and he held me very close before he drove away and just said, 'Thank you, darling!' But his gratitude wrapped round me like a warm cloak and eased the pain of our first separation.

There had been a case of measles at the girls' boarding school. I wondered if Lillian might have caught it, but the local doctor who called to see her that afternoon shook his head.

'Lillian often runs these temperatures, Mrs Rivers,' he told me. 'All three girls are very highly-strung and when they get overwrought, this is the way they react. It's nature's cure, you know. It forces them to go to bed and remain quiet.'

I had liked the young dark-haired Yorkshireman on sight. Now I felt that he was an excellent doctor. Although he was young he seemed well qualified to deal with children. I took him down to the drawing room for a glass of sherry and he introduced himself more fully.

'My name is Robert Carnes,' he said, his Yorkshire accent only just discernible. 'I'm in partnership with Dr Williams, but he is semi-retired now. I took over the Rivers family two years ago. May I congratulate you on your marriage? I'm sure having you here will make a great difference to the children.'

His manner was warm and friendly, and he was not unattractive with dark, deep-set eyes and a tousle of black hair which gave him a boyish appearance. A year ago I might well have described him to Joanne as highly interesting and a possible boyfriend. Now, married to Cam and so much in love, other men, even charming intelligent young men like this doctor, left me immune. But I liked him.

'Why should Lillian be overwrought?' I asked him as we sipped our sherry.

He shrugged his shoulders. 'You should know that better than I,' he said. 'Maybe because she knew her father was going away – or thought you were going? Children have many illogical as well as logical fears, you know. I'm particularly interested in child psychology and want to specialise in it. Of course, in this case one must bear in mind the shock all three children received when their mother died. I was not in Yorkshire at the time, but Dr Williams put me in the picture.'

'But Lillian was only five when it happened!'

'Old enough to be aware of tragedy. And who knows what she has heard since? Village people talk. Mrs Meadows may have gossiped unwisely. Naturally, everyone tried to keep the details of the late Mrs Rivers' death from the younger children, but they do know she was drowned in the lake. You may have noticed none of them will go near it.'

I shook my head. Since that day of our arrival, the weather had suddenly changed and a thick, cold mist had hung about the house and garden, completely obliterating the hills behind and making outdoor activities unwelcome. Cam and I had taken the children to the town eight miles away, to the cinema, and they had come to the village shopping with me, but no one had felt inclined to play in the garden and we had spent a great deal of time in the nursery.

Dr Carnes stood up, putting his empty glass on the table. 'I know Lillian is very happy that you haven't gone to London after all. She told me so. You may well find that by tomorrow her temperature will be down. Meanwhile, rest, quiet, and Dispirin every four hours for the headache and to help her sleep.'

After the young doctor had left, I went back upstairs toward Lillian's room. Muriel came out as I approached. She saw me and put her finger to her lips.

'She's sleeping.' she told me. 'I thought if I read to her for a little while, she'd probably drop off, and she has.'

'That was kind of you, Muriel.' I said. I followed her back downstairs wondering why I had been unable to get close to her as I had to the other children. She had been so very helpful and considerate – perhaps a little too obvious in her efforts to keep the younger children out of Cam's and my way – but she meant well and I was grateful. I found her very reserved. I seemed unable to get through the barrier. It was almost as if she were deliberately keeping me at bay. I reminded myself that her reserve was natural. I was, in a way, an interloper in this house – the newcomer. She was a part of it, had grown up here. I must give her time to get used to me.

'Cam tells me you paint.' I said. 'If you would ever like to show your work to me, I'd love to see it. I don't have much knowledge of painting, but I am interested, especially in modern art.'

Muriel gave me a long, searching look. 'I doubt you'd like my efforts,' she said. 'Father thinks they are depressing.'

'A great deal in life is sad,' I said. 'I quite see why an artist should feel the need to portray sadness as well as happiness.'

Muriel hesitated a moment longer; then, her mind made up, she said abruptly, 'I was just going over to the studio. Come and look if you like.'

I felt a little thrill of satisfaction. At last I seemed to be making headway with Muriel.

I followed her along an old brick path on the north side of the house, leading first through the shrubbery, then over a cobbled yard around which there were empty stables.

There was something dreary about this forsaken yard, the weeds pushing up through the stones, the windows dusty and covered in spider webs. Muriel, moving lightly and gracefully, led me through one of the stable doors into a long dark room smelling faintly of old leather and horses.

We walked past the rows of empty stalls into what had been a saddle and harness room, then up a narrow curved staircase.

Suddenly we were in a huge vaulted loft which had been skilfully converted.

Muriel's studio was much as I had imagined such a room would be, facing north, with a vast skylight, canvases stacked high against every wall, and one, covered by a cloth, on an easel. A divan, daubed with paint spots, was littered with sheets of drawing paper covered with pencil sketches.

The girl was watching my face with interest as I stared around. She moved past me and began to turn one or two of the canvases to face me. Several were so abstract that they were quite meaningless to me with their dark blobs of black, brown, and violet paint and streaks of scarlet that looked like raw wounds. I repressed a shudder. I could well see why Cam didn't care for them.

Suddenly my eye was caught by a really beautiful painting of the lake.

'Why, it's our lake!' I cried. 'Oh, Muriel, it's lovely!'

It was, to me anyway, a real work of art. Somehow she had caught the sunlight on the water so that it shimmered and danced before the eyes. To one side, the overhanging trees cast deep, cold shadows contrasting perfectly and accentuating the brightness of the water. Looking at the other side, you could almost hear the waterfall as it tumbled over a rocky crag and splashed into the deep green and white water beneath.

'It's lovely!' I said again. 'Has Cam seen it? I'm sure he'd want us to hang it in the house. How clever of you, Muriel.'

She seemed quite unmoved by my praise. 'It has a great many technical faults,' she said critically. 'Besides, Father would hardly want a reminder of the very spot where Jennifer was drowned. She slipped over the waterfall, you know, and crushed her skull on the stones. There are sharp rocks below the water – that's why it looks such a dark green compared with the other side of the lake.'

Once again I was shocked. I realised that the girl was giving a factual explanation of her painting and was therefore unaware of the impact her calm description of Jennifer's terrible death would have upon me. Like all artists, she was immersed in her art. But I was not. I felt ashamed of my own tactlessness in suggesting that the painting should be hung in the house. I should have remembered Jennifer's tragedy.

To hide my embarrassment I turned away and pointed to the canvas on the easel. 'May I see that?' I asked tentatively.

Muriel shrugged as if she didn't care one way or the other and lifted the cloth. I found myself staring at my own portrait.

There was no doubt that it was *me* – but as I stood there staring at it, I realised that Muriel had caught only a part of me. She had re-created me as a starry-eyed, glowing, innocent young bride. I looked far younger than my twenty-four years with the open happy face of a child – trusting, simple, uncomplicated – almost stupid.

I felt myself blushing without knowing why. I could not possibly object to such a portrait. Feature by feature the likeness was exact; my colouring perfect. It was only my expression... well, maybe Muriel had seen me looking that way at Cam. With him I did feel young and starry-eyed and trusting and happy.

'Don't you like it?' Muriel said at my elbow, startling me. I smiled with an effort.

'I think you flatter me, Muriel. I'm not really as young as you have made me look.'

'That's how I see you,' Muriel said quietly.

'Without vices of any kind?'

She turned away so that I could not see her face. '*Do* you have any?' she countered.

'Perhaps not. But I can be very determined, Muriel, and quite hard at times. I have had to fend for myself since I was fifteen, and I am well used to taking care of myself. If I want anything badly enough, I will leave no stone unturned to get it; nor, once having got it, would I let it go without a fight.'

'You surprise me,' Muriel replied. 'I wouldn't have thought of you as a fighter exactly. It's interesting, isn't it? How one sees only part of a person. People are like icebergs with five-sixths of themselves hidden from view; perhaps the dangerous part of them is out of sight,' she added thoughtfully.

'But you ought not to feel like that, Muriel,' I argued impulsively. 'People on the whole are good and kind and decent. You're quite wrong in supposing that the hidden side is evil.'

'It depends how you define good and evil,' Muriel replied enigmatically. 'Personally, I think most people are extraordinarily silly. They meander through life without any real purpose. One must have a design for living if a life is to mean anything. Don't you agree?'

'Yes, I suppose so,' I said. I felt out of my depth. I presumed Muriel's purpose in life was her art. I was surprised that Cam had not told me of her considerable talent. But then he never did talk much about her.

'What is your true purpose in life?' Muriel persisted. 'But perhaps that is none of my business. All the same, I can't help wondering *why* you married my stepfather.'

Once again Muriel had succeeded in completely throwing me off balance. But this, at least, I could answer without reflection. 'Because I fell in love with him. Why else?'

Muriel smiled. 'Well, he *is* a very rich man,' she said lightly, factually. Though the remark might be insulting, the tone was totally innocent. 'And he's so much older than you and with so many stepdaughters, it was quite noble if you married him just for love.'

Now at last I felt I could talk to her. 'You won't feel that way once you fall in love,' I told her. 'Then you'll understand. There was nothing in the least noble about my intentions. They were entirely selfish. I loved Cam and wanted to spend my life with him. Nothing else mattered.'

'You might not have said that if he'd been very poor and lived in a bad neighbourhood on a mere pittance.'

I tried to imagine such a situation and said truthfully, 'I don't think it would have made any difference, Muriel. I love your father, and I would have been very happy to marry him even in the conditions you suggest.'

'Then you've never been really poor!' Muriel said, and before I could argue with her, added, 'Of course, he isn't my real father – I expect you know that.'

I nodded, waiting for her to continue but she covered my portrait and said, 'Well, I suppose it is nearly supper time. We'd better go back to the house.'

I took my dismissal cheerfully. After all, this was Muriel's private domain, and I tried to feel privileged that she had brought me in the first place. Yet, looking back on it, it seemed more as if she had meant to confuse and puzzle me by that curious portrait of myself. I felt guilty for harbouring such a thought. The mere fact that she had considered me worth painting was in itself a compliment.

But as I walked through the old stable yard back toward the house, I could not altogether rid myself of the uneasy feeling that Muriel had been mocking me when she showed me that spectacular painting of myself. I *did* look stupid in it, an ingénue with half-open lips and a soulful expression in my eyes. I felt more and more certain that the sophisticated Muriel – so much older than her years, so complex – must have been laughing at me, intent on ridiculing me. I wished now that I had never gone along to the studio, but because of my deep love for Cam I reproached myself for allowing even the smallest suspicion of Muriel to take root. I determined there and then to try harder to understand her – to trust her motives, no matter what she did, and accept her as I did the smaller girls – as a stepdaughter I loved and whom I believed would come to love me.

We ate supper – a light meal of omelettes and fruit jellies – in the big dining room in strange silence. Sandra and Debbie seemed subdued – as if their father's absence was depressing them as well as me. How different it was when Cam was here – everyone talking and laughing and even the stammering Sandra joining in the conversation as well as she was able. I wished I had thought to tell Mrs Meadows we would eat in the nursery, and resolved that we would do so tomorrow, and every night until the weekend when Cam was due home.

Outside the house the mist had been washed away by a heavy downpour of rain which fell in a relentless sheet. The sky looked dark and menacing. I shivered, wondering if I had caught a cold. Hurriedly I drew the curtains and switched on more lights. Despite the presence of the children, I felt indescribably lonely and depressed. I wished desperately that Cam would walk into the room and put his arms around me. The two-bar electric fire did not seem capable of taking the chill from the room and when Mrs Meadows came in to clear the pudding plates away, I told her I would take my coffee in the nursery.

Debbie swung round in her chair, her face suddenly glowing. 'With us?' she said. 'Oh, good! Will you stay and play with us? Please, Kate, please!'

'Don't be such a pest, Debbie!' Muriel said sharply. 'Kate will have things of her own to do.'

'But of course not!' I said, putting an arm around Debbie's shoulders. 'This is just the night for a nice cosy evening round the nursery fire.'

'S-s-super!' said Sandra, coming round the table to cling to my hand.

'But I must look in on Lillian first,' I told them, happy that they should want me.

I peeped into the darkened room – a pretty room with blue and white chintzes and nursery wallpaper. The cupboards were crammed with Lillian's toys – but also filled now with shadows as I peered towards the bed. There was no movement, and I imagined the child was still sleeping. It occurred to me that if she woke up in total darkness she might be afraid, so I switched on the tiny bedside light. As I did so a shaky little voice said, 'Oh, *thank* you, Kate!' as if I had done an immense kindness.

'So you are awake after all,' I said, sitting down on Lillian's bed and smoothing the hair from her hot, damp forehead.

'I'm not woken up. I haven't been to sleep,' she said.

I smiled. 'But you were, you know. Muriel said you were fast asleep when she looked in earlier.'

Suddenly the child's arms were clasped round my neck and I felt the thin eight-year-old body trembling against my own. Hot tears splashed down on my hands.

'Poor darling, you aren't feeling very well, are you?' I said gently. 'I tell you what – we'll change your nightie and remake the bed. Then you have a nice cool wash and I'll ask Mrs Meadows to bring you up something special to eat. How would that be?'

Lillian only sobbed harder and clung to me more fiercely. 'Now be a good girl,' I said, trying to disentangle her arms. 'You'll only put your temperature up.'

'But I'm frightened!' Lillian wept against my neck. 'Promise you won't go away. Promise!'

'But there's nothing at all to be frightened of,' I said as calmly as I could. 'Did you have a bad dream, darling? Is that it?'

It was some minutes before I was able to make out that Lillian's fear was of ghosts. 'They come in the dark!' she sobbed. 'I know they do. I've *seen* them!'

It took me some time to calm her down. I thought it best not to take her fears too seriously. To ask the identity of her 'ghosts' might lend them a reality I very much hoped to dispel. I just told her gently that they were only in her imagination since ghosts did not exist.

'But they do – they do!' Lillian protested. 'Debbie and Sandy've seen them, too.'

'She has these fits of hysteria – she's very highly-strung.' Muriel's voice coming unexpectedly from the doorway startled us both. I certainly jumped nearly as much as Lillian.

'It's best really to ignore it. If you take her seriously, she just gets worse,' Muriel said calmly. 'Now you lie down and be a good girl, Lillian. Understand? It's not fair to upset poor Kate in this way. You don't want to upset her, do you?'

'No.' Lillian's voice was a trembling murmur. 'But I don't want to be in the dark, Muriel, please!'

'Well, of course not, silly!' Muriel said, loosening Lillian's grip on me and laying her gently back on the pillows. 'I'd have put the light on for you if I'd thought you were awake.'

Calmly, efficiently, she straightened Lillian's bed and, I had to admit, managed to quieten Lillian in a way that I'd obviously not succeeded in doing. I went downstairs to see to Lillian's supper – she wanted only soup – and when I returned Lillian showed no sign of her earlier hysteria. Mrs

Meadows had said she would sit with her for a while so, at Muriel's suggestion, we left the room to go back to the other children.

As we walked along the passage, Muriel said, 'I expect you'll get used to dealing with children when you've been here a bit longer. Dr Carnes told Father they were all three neurotic, but I don't think Father understood what he was talking about. I daresay the shock of Jennifer's death was a bit much for them. They are all afraid of the dark and ghosts and such like. I sometimes think they'd all be a lot better away from this house, and Dr Carnes agrees with me, but Father won't hear of it. He says they are away nine months of the year at school, and the short time they are home can't do them any harm.'

How sensible Muriel was, I thought. But then she had more or less had to be a mother to the girls for the past three years. It was natural that she understood them better than I did. She had spoken a little more sternly to Lillian than I would have done, but not unkindly, and Lillian had reacted favourably at once.

'I do appreciate your help, Muriel,' I said gratefully, 'I do so want them to be happy.'

'Of course,' said Muriel as she opened the nursery door. 'Those were Father's words, too.'

Oh, Cam! I thought as his two little girls came running across the room towards me. I hope I won't make a mess of this job. I want to be a good mother to them.

I'd have given a great deal at that moment to see my husband come into the room.

He did telephone me later, when I was in bed, partly to inquire after Lillian but mainly to say how much he missed me and how much he loved me.

His call relaxed and soothed me. After a last peep at Lillian, who was sleeping soundly, her face peaceful and less flushed in the small circle of illumination that came from the night light, I fell asleep.

I'm not quite sure what time it was when I awoke. The room was pitch dark and for a moment I forgot that Cam was not beside me and reached over to his side of the bed. Then, still drowsy with sleep, I remembered he was in London and was almost asleep again when I heard a cry. At first I though it was an owl, but a moment later I was sure it was a child. I listened, holding my breath, but the cry was not repeated. I was still trying to make up my mind if I had imagined it when I heard footsteps outside my door. There was a faint knock and then the door creaked open.

'Are you awake, Kate?'

'Oh, Muriel, it's you. Come in.'

'I thought you might have been worried by the crying. I just came to tell you it was only Debbie having one of her nightmares.'

'Debbie?' I repeated, still stupid with sleep.

'Yes. She's quite all right now. I thought you might like to know. Goodnight.'

It was only when Muriel had closed the door behind her that I came fully awake. I sat up, switched on my bedside light and brushed the hair out of my eyes. My bedside clock said it was two a.m. Poor Muriel, I thought, doing night duty as well as day. I must make more effort to look after the children myself. It wasn't right that a girl only eighteen years of age should have to be mother to three half-sisters.

I resolved to speak to Cam about it on his return. He might think Muriel was quite happy here with her painting and her studio, but she ought to be out and about with other young people. Where was young Logan, for instance? I'd been at Quarry House over two weeks and had not seen him yet. I'd suggest to Muriel in the morning that she invite him to lunch that very day. Come to think of it, I'd not yet met any of Cam's friends. Obviously he must know people in the district, although we had no near neighbours. It was strange that no one had called. Perhaps word had not yet reached them that Cam had a new wife.

We'd been married very quietly in a London Registry Office with only Joanne and a business colleague of Cam's as witnesses. It was, after all, Cam's third marriage, and I understood and approved his wish to keep the ceremony as private as possible. Only now did I feel a little hurt that he had not at least let his circle of family friends know of my existence.

But I soon quelled this feeling. We were both so much in love we didn't really want to be bothered with other people's company. With our ready-made family, we had all we needed. But Muriel did need more, and I intended to see she had the opportunity to entertain her young man if she wished.

Chapter Four

Lillian's temperature had risen again in the night. By morning her little face was flushed with fever and there were huge dark rings under her eyes. Muriel said she thought it unnecessary to ask Dr Carnes to call again but by lunch time, when Lillian seemed no better, I decided to play safe.

The doctor waved aside my apologies. 'Of course I'll come, Mrs Rivers. You're quite justified in calling me if you're worried. Please don't hesitate to do so whenever you wish.'

I had not met many Yorkshire people but I thought that if the young doctor and Mrs Meadows were typical examples, I was going to like them very much. There was a warmth and friendliness about them which one did not find very often these days in London.

Mrs Meadows was a wonderful woman – industrious and good-tempered. While Cam was at home I hadn't found much time to talk to her but this morning, as I gave her a hand making beds and cleaning the nursery, we became firm friends. She was a fount of information about the local inhabitants, many of whom were interrelated, and all the families seemed to have lived in the locality for centuries.

Strangers, as she called them, had moved into nearby towns, mostly to new housing developments which had not yet spread as far as our village. She had nothing good to say about modernisation of the old life-style and resented anything that spelled change from the days of her youth. Hardworking, of farming stock, she was the epitome of what we Londoners called 'the salt of the earth' – a superb cook, responsible, honest, and undemanding except for her insistence that standards should never be dropped. She led an organised self-disciplined life and her loyalty to the family was total.

We had a snack together at the kitchen table and she expanded her views. 'When Muriel told me her father was marrying a young girl, I was worried, I was!' she told me confidentially. 'I thought to myself you'd be one of those London flibbertigibbets. But you're not a bit like that. I'm more than happy you've come. Mr Rivers is often away, and the responsibility for the young ones is more than I feel able to manage.'

Mrs Meadows poured out two more cups of tea and gave me a quick, embarrassed glance.

'Maybe I shouldn't say this, but I feel it's my duty,' she said. 'If it weren't for the little girls, I'd have given in my notice long ago. Mr Meadows doesn't care at all for me working here. He'd like for us to leave the cottage and get a new house in the village.'

'Well, I can understand that,' I told her. 'Not everyone wants to live in a small cottage. But your husband has been gardener here a long while, hasn't he? Wouldn't he be sorry to leave such a beautiful place?'

'That he would!' agreed the plump little woman, 'but he'd rather leave than have me stay in this house.'

Something in her tone made me look at her sharply. 'This house?' I repeated.

She nodded. 'It's got a bad name,' she said softly. 'And you can't wonder at that.'

I sighed. It wasn't difficult to understand that, with two tragedies in thirteen years, Quarry House had acquired a reputation for bad luck. Yorkshire people were not particularly superstitious, but no doubt in the village there were some people simple enough to believe, like little Lillian, in ghosts.

'You don't believe the house is haunted, do you, Mrs Meadows?' I asked, curious to see her reaction.

She neither affirmed nor denied my question. Her face seemed to close up and she rapidly changed the conversation to Muriel. 'I know she's had a hard life in some ways and that no doubt accounts for her manner, but she's that haughty I sometimes wonder why I put up with it. Do this! Do that! She orders me when all she need do is ask. Why, I knew her when she was a little girl living with our Mrs Grant by the Post Office. Wild little thing she was in those days. Mrs Grant couldn't manage her and had to ask Mr Rivers to make other arrangements. Couldn't seem to mix in with Mrs Grant's children and always stood apart, shut up inside herself. She hasn't changed.'

'Poor Muriel,' I said. 'She's been such a help to me with the younger ones. She seems to be able to manage them wonderfully well.'

'Perhaps not everyone would agree with you,' said Mrs Meadows darkly. 'They're that frightened of her. I always say it isn't good for children to be ruled by fear.'

'But she doesn't do that,' I said. 'I've seen her be firm with them, but never once has she been unkind in any way. I'm sure you're mistaken, Mrs Meadows.'

She turned away and began to wash up the tea things. I could sense that I would be wasting my time trying to argue with her. Clearly she and Muriel were up against each other. It wasn't difficult to see how such a situation had come about. Muriel's reserve and self-assurance didn't exactly endear her to people. I found it difficult to like her myself.

In a thoughtful frame of mind, I went upstairs to sit with Lillian. When Muriel and I became better friends, perhaps I could talk to her – explain that a gentler, more friendly approach to the housekeeper might pay dividends.

I was still with Lillian when Dr Carnes arrived. I thought again how pleasant his manner was with the child and what a very likeable person he was. It was difficult to judge his age, but I guessed he was twenty-eight, possibly thirty at the most. Lillian obviously adored him and begged him impulsively to stay to tea with her.

'Well, it would be very nice,' he accepted, after I had endorsed Lillian's request. 'I can't remember when I last had tea in a young lady's bedroom!'

He grinned across the bed at me and I found myself laughing. Lillian laughed, too, although she could not have understood the implication of his remark.

That afternoon I found out a great deal about Robert Carnes and I liked all that I discovered. His parents had come of mining stock, and his father had spent all his life in the pits. Robert, the only son, had determined to make something more of his life and had worked his way up the educational spiral, ending with a scholarship to Edinburgh University to study medicine. There hadn't been much time for fun in the proverbial sense of the word, but he had enjoyed the struggle. He would have liked to stay on at college to take further examinations in child psychology, but because of poverty and the self-sacrifices his parents had made to help him qualify, he felt he owed it to them to start earning a living.

'Now I study at night,' he said, 'when I can find time. One day I will specialise in children.'

I didn't doubt it. There was a quality about him which made one feel totally confident in his ability to achieve anything he had set his heart on. Yet, at the same time, he wasn't hard or calculating – only ambitious. He had a quick sense of humour which I liked, and it was only as I shared the enjoyment of laughter with him that I realised how little I had smiled since Cam had left the house. Somehow, with Cam away, the atmosphere had become heavy, oppressive – almost threatening. But it was not so in Lillian's room that afternoon. Perhaps we should have stayed quieter since the child was feverish, but far from doing her any harm, she looked a great deal better when finally Robert rose to go. We had soon found the formality of surnames too tiresome for easy exchange of ideas and conversation, and being much of an age, we had quickly drifted into the use of first names.

Muriel had taken the other girls out for a walk in the hills, the weather having improved since the heavy rain. They came in through the front door just as Robert was going. Debbie and Sandra ran to greet him as if he were an old friend. Muriel remained beautiful and still, looking at our laughing faces with what I can only describe as faint disapproval – as if we were a group of badly behaved youngsters who ought to know better.

I went across and linked my arm in hers. 'We've had such a nice tea party with Lillian,' I told her, trying to draw her into the group, 'I wish you could have been with us.'

She did not reply but gently detached my arm from hers, said a polite 'good afternoon' to Robert and then collected the two girls, telling them to go and change out of their muddy clothes at once. She sounded more like their governess than their half-sister.

It was only after Robert had gone that I remembered I had intended to ask Logan over for the day. I felt guilty about it. I told myself I really must concentrate more on Muriel and less on her sisters.

On Friday Lillian was up and about and I insisted, brooking no argument, that Muriel devote the day to her own pursuits. Sensing my determination, she gave in – not very graciously, but with a half smile with which I was content.

'Very well, I'll telephone Logan and invite him for lunch.' I told Mrs Meadows to prepare something especially nice, but when she heard for whom the meal was to be cooked, she shook her head and said, 'That good-for-nothing! Mr Rivers doesn't care for him, nor more do I. Long-haired, flibbertigibbet!'

I laughed. It was clearly one of Mrs Meadows' favourite descriptions for people she didn't like.

I knew from Mrs Meadows that Logan Winter was crossbreeding Welsh-Arab ponies on the neighbouring farm. 'An impoverished gentleman farmer', she described him with a trace of sarcasm on the word 'gentleman'. His old father was bedridden after two strokes, and his mother had died some years back, so I had a brief idea of his background. The word 'impoverished' puzzled me. Surely, I thought, breeding horses must be quite an expensive pastime? As far as I knew, Muriel herself did not ride. I wondered whether she was thinking seriously about marrying Logan and how she would like a life tied up with horses. Somehow she did not seem to me to be an outdoor girl, although there was a certain wildness beneath the calm surface. I remembered that as a little girl she had run wild in these hills.

When I finally met Logan, I realised that my speculations on a marriage between him and Muriel were unnecessary. There seemed little affection between them. They spoke to one another rather as a brother and sister might do, familiarly but without intimacy. Frankly, I was glad. I didn't like the young man any more than Mrs Meadows did and I could well understand why Cam had not taken to him. It was not so much on account of his appearance. In fact, in riding breeches and a yellow sweater, he did not look in the least foppish but was quite attractive. It was, I think, his eyes and his mouth I found objectionable – the first a hard, glittering blue, ice-cold like aquamarines; and the latter full and loose and weak. A complicated mixture, I decided, after studying him.

He was not exactly rude, but he certainly did not set out to charm me – I suppose he had no cause to do so. Nor did I see any significant glances between him and Muriel; he made no attempt to touch her, or, come to that, to charm her either. The only link which seemed to exist between them was the occasional brief ironic look they exchanged when I made some casual remark – as if they were sharing a joke at the fatuousness of my conversation. I felt my temper rising. I didn't intend to have Logan – a guest, after all, in my house – laughing at me up his sleeve and encouraging Muriel to do likewise. In a strange way which puzzled me, I thought them too much alike. They had the same brooding, unsmiling countenances.

It was quite by chance that I discovered they were, in fact, distantly related. Logan gave me this information when we were having coffee in the drawing room. I gathered from his conversation to Muriel that she was painting a portrait of his mother from a snapshot he had given her, and he wanted to know if she had finished it yet.

'I'm finding it difficult, Logan,' Muriel replied. 'I become confused – she was so like my own mother.'

'Well, they were alike, weren't they?' was Logan's reply. Seeing that I was listening, he said, 'They were cousins, you know.' and thus explained his relationship to Muriel.

I felt suddenly lost – as if I had awakened in the middle of a dream, finding myself halfway along a road without knowing how I had arrived there. I really knew nothing but the bare facts about Cam's past life. Now I found myself consumed with curiosity. What kind of woman had the first Mrs Rivers been? Like Muriel? I did not even know this much. Had Cam once been in love with her? Was it ever between them the way it was now between Cam and myself?

Jealousy held me briefly in its cold embrace until I reminded myself that Cam had told me he had never known the meaning of love before he met me. Then why had he married her, I asked myself uneasily.

My knowledge of the second Mrs Rivers – Jennifer – was greater. I knew her first name, that she had been nanny to the orphaned Muriel, and that Cam had married her as much for convenience as for anything else. She had been a good wife and a good mother. The little girls had a large framed photograph of her in the nursery and once again the round, smiling face had struck me as pleasant, and kind. I'm sure I would have liked her.

But about Muriel's mother I knew nothing, other than that she was quite a few years older than Cam at the time of their marriage. I knew if Joanne were with me she would caution me to stop probing into the past.

'What's done is done!' was one of her favourite remarks. And I agreed with her. But now I felt a desperate need to fill in those long years of Cam's life which I had been unable to share with him.

With the coffee finished, Muriel suggested taking Logan over to the studio. Remembering my intention to keep the younger girls out of her way, I told Debbie and Sandra to run upstairs and get ready to go for a walk. Though it was cold, the sun was shining and I didn't think it would harm Lillian to go with us.

Outside in the garden old Meadows was burning leaves. The blue-grey smoke filled the air with a wonderful pungent scent and when my three young stepdaughters started to whoop and toss the fallen leaves in the air, I felt like doing the same. We mutually abandoned the idea of a walk and found rakes and brooms and helped Meadows with his bonfire. Within no time at all, the girls' faces were rosy and happy, and you could have heard their shouts of laughter way down in the valley.

Meadows said something to me in such a broad Yorkshire accent, that I didn't understand it. But as he stood leaning on his broom, scratching his nearly bald head, his eyes were warm and friendly. He pointed to the children and then at me and nodded his head. I think he was trying to tell me that I was good for them, or that he approved of the way I was letting them run around like little wild things.

I stood leaning against the trunk of a vast beech tree watching the old gardener light a cigarette butt he'd taken from behind his ear and smoke slowly until there was nothing left to hold between his lips. We were silent, but it was a companionable silence, broken by the shouts of the children and the crackling of the dry leaves as they flared to flames every now and then. I felt my earlier depression lighten and vanish. I was happy despite Cam's absence, though sad, too, because he couldn't share this moment with me.

No wonder he loved Quarry House. I could well understand his attachment to the place, especially since he had grown up here himself. Could Meadows have been gardener here when Cam was a boy, tossing leaves on the bonfire? It was possible.

I felt the first tugs of family continuity. I suddenly understood why Cam wanted a son. One day all his girls would marry and leave home. A boy would bring his wife back here, just as Cam had brought me. I would give Cam a son – soon, I thought. I mustn't wait too long or he would be too old really to enjoy him. When the time came I would pray that it was a boy! Cam certainly didn't need any more daughters. If it's a girl, I'll leave it on someone's doorstep, I thought, smiling to myself for I'd never be able to do such a thing in a million years, or drown it in the lake!

Quite suddenly I wasn't smiling any longer. My day-dreaming had been entirely inconsequential – no more than a lazy, contented glimpse into the future. But suddenly my thoughts had run away with my consciousness and I was tied up with the past. What a horrible, revolting idea, I told myself, shocked. To joke about drowning a baby in the lake was quite unpardonable. How had such an idea entered my mind?

I turned to look at the lake and shivered. The breeze was rippling the grey water so that it was ridged like sand after the tide had receded. The surrounding trees waved their branches slowly, like ballet dancers in a macabre dance sequence.

It was there, I remembered with horror, that poor Jennifer had drowned. I knew nothing about the accident beyond the few stark facts Muriel had told me, which were horrifying enough for me not to want to know the details. I could well understand Cam's reluctance to talk of his former marriage.

I gave myself a mental shake. If I wasn't careful, I was going to let the past creep up on me and make me neurotic. I walked away from Meadows and across the lawn to the little Victorian summer-house. It had never been used as such. In Cam's childhood it was a repository for tennis racquets, cricket bats, and fishing rods. Now it was empty except for a scatter of fallen leaves which had blown in through the cracked windowpane. Everywhere, the once-white paint had peeled in strips.

Suddenly I had an idea. I called the girls over to me and asked them if they would like to convert this into their own Wendy house. They were excited and enchanted by the idea, and I wondered why no one had thought of it before.

'It'll be ours, just for ourselves,' Debbie said, clapping her hands. 'It will, won't it, Kate? Not even Muriel shall come in.'

'I was perturbed by the tone of her voice, it was so vehement. I told myself it was a natural childish instinct to wish to exclude adults – even Muriel, who probably seemed like a grown-up to these children.

'No, none of us will come near,' I promised. Suddenly a warm sticky hand was thrust into mine.

'B-b-but w-we w-w-want you, K-k-kate!' Poor Sandra with her acute stutter found it easier as a rule not to try to talk. I was very touched, especially when her two sisters eagerly endorsed her wish.

'Well, we can't just exclude Muriel,' I told them gently. 'She would be very hurt to be the only one left out and you wouldn't want to hurt her feelings, would you?'

Nobody spoke. I felt caught in a trap of my own making and was wondering how to extricate myself when Debbie said, 'We aren't allowed in her studio so it would be *fair* not to let her in our house!'

Childish justice. At least it served as an excuse for Muriel's exclusion – one I could put to her in the right way.

'So!' I said smiling. 'And what will you call your new house?'

All three bubbled with suggestions. In the end, they decided to call it Kitten Cottage, because, explained Lillian, 'Daddy once found a stray kitten in here when he was a little boy.'

I had not thought of Cam for several hours. Now my heart began to sing at the thought that he would be with us tomorrow. It would make him happy to see how happy we were, his children and I, in each other's company. We needed only him with us to complete our magic circle.

Happiness welled up inside me, a feeling so intense that I had a stupid urge to cry. I'd never really had a family. An only child is lonely, no matter how much its parents love it.

We had almost finished tea before I realised that Muriel and Logan had not come to join us. I don't think any of us missed them – the children certainly never mentioned their absence and I had totally forgotten them.

I sighed. Poor Muriel! Beautiful, capable, self-reliant, and talented though she was, I was finding it very hard to like her. I felt it was my responsibility to break down the barriers I did not fully understand that were of her making. I really wanted to draw her into the family circle. I believed that ultimately I would succeed so that there would be no unhappiness or loneliness in Quarry House.

Chapter Five

I was so happy to have Cam back again that for a few hours after his return I could think of little else. It was all either of us could do to give the children the attention they demanded. When we finally escaped to our bedroom, Cam took me in his arms and said fiercely, 'I'm never ever going away again without you, Kate. It's been so damned lonely.'

'Well, I haven't had all that much time to miss you!' I teased him, kissing him between each word. 'I've been far too busy with your family.'

'I'm jealous. You've stopped loving me.'

He held me tightly against him and I closed my eyes. This was somehow a different Cam – more possessive, more intense.

'I love you more than ever each day that goes by,' I told him truthfully. 'I'll never stop loving you.'

The love that existed between Cam and me was a strange emotion, I thought. It was like a current of electricity flowing between us, becoming magnified and increased by such simple little things as words, smiles, kisses. I knew that our love could never be a static thing – it would either grow more wonderful or shrivel up and die. In a way we were still virtual strangers. There was so much I still had to learn about Cam – and he about me. This voyage of discovery was a wonderfully new and exciting thing for me. Later, when our physical need for one another had been satisfied, I could not help but wonder, as I lay at peace in Cam's embrace, whether he felt as I did – that our love was unique. I wanted to ask him but forbore from doing so, in case he thought I was jealous of those years he had shared with other women. I was, too! I believed him when he said he had not loved either of them, but the cold fact remained he had been a husband to two other women before me – this lover who should have been all mine. The primitive feminine side of my nature was rising to the surface. Now, for the first time, with the growing intensity of my emotions, I found myself wishing that that past had never been.

His fingers gently traced the curve of my bare shoulder. I looked down into his eyes and he smiled up at me, sleepy, loving, at peace.

'Oh, Cam,' I whispered, without quite knowing what it was I wanted to tell him.

'I love you, too!' he whispered. 'Now and always, darling.' Some while later, when we were dressing for supper, I told him about the days he'd been away. He was in full approval of my calling in Robert Carnes, although, he added smilingly, 'I'd prefer a little less of the "Robert" and a little more of the "doctor" in your conversation.'

I laughed. 'Are you jealous?'

'Should I be?'

I pushed the electric razor away from his chin and kissed him quickly. 'Perhaps a little. He's very attractive.'

I had not meant Cam to take me seriously, but he did. His voice was stiff as he said tartly, 'He's young, too – the right age for you.'

'Oh, *darling*!' I cried, shocked that he could even think that way. Yet hadn't I also thought of Robert in terms of a boyfriend who might have appealed to me in the old days when I shared a flat with Joanne? 'That's too silly,' I said. 'I won't even discuss it.'

Cam resumed shaving, his eyes thoughtful. 'I still can't believe you're my wife,' he said a moment later. 'You're so very young, my darling, and so very attractive. I can't understand what you see in me – what advantage there could possibly be for you in our marriage. Quite apart from my age, there are all my daughters. In my heart, I know you should have something far better than I can give you.'

'Cam!' I said quietly. 'I love you. If you were yet another ten years older, I wouldn't care. As to the girls, I'm beginning to love them, too.'

I found myself telling him enthusiastically about the summer-house, going into far greater detail than could possibly interest him. It was only on later reflection that I realised I was just putting off the moment when I must discuss Muriel with him.

The children calling us down to supper saved me but I knew I could not put it off indefinitely. I plucked up courage when we went to bed that night.

'She's so very difficult to like,' I tried to explain to him. 'It makes her odd-man-out, and she must be very unhappy and lonely. She's so reserved, Cam, that I find it almost impossible to get inside the barrier she puts around herself. She doesn't seem really to care about anything – unless it's her painting.'

I paused and then went on to tell him about Muriel's portrait of me. But I knew I wasn't making sense. I didn't even know myself what had upset me about the portrait. Whenever I thought about it, I felt insulted but there wasn't one single logical reason *why* I should feel that way.

Cam heard me out and then said, 'Well, I know she's difficult, darling, but I think you're worrying far too much about her. She's always been reserved. It's just her nature. As to her manner with the children, she has always managed them most capably. I honestly can't believe she ever gives them cause to be *frightened* of her, though I admit she's strict. But they can be little monkeys, and they need a firm hand. I've always thought Muriel was pretty efficient with them.'

'Yes, I know,' I said sighing, 'but she isn't their mother or their governess. I'm not saying I could manage them better, if as well, but I do feel I ought to take them off her hands – for her sake as well as theirs.'

Cam climbed into bed and lay watching me as I sat at the dressing table brushing my hair. 'Aren't you content to have just me on your hands?' he asked smiling.

I remained silent. Of course I wanted nothing more than to be able to devote myself completely to Cam. But I couldn't ignore the fact that he had three daughters whom I was beginning to love. I had not thought of myself as primarily maternal, but somehow his children had touched my heart – Lillian with her feverish, tear-stained little face begging me to stay with her because of the 'ghosts' – Debbie's grubby little hand tucked into mine down by the summer-house – Sandra's halting, stammering voice trying to communicate.

I realised that Cam, who no doubt over the years had come to accept things as they were, perhaps did not react to their motherlessness the way I, a newcomer, was doing. Like most males, he was content to let things run on as they were since there was no disruption of his personal life. Really, I told myself, it was Cam, their father, who should be anxious about them – not me!

'Still worrying?' Cam asked as I climbed into bed and snuggled down beside him.

'A little,' I answered truthfully.

'Well, don't!' said Cam. 'Worry about me!'

He didn't give me a chance then to do otherwise. Nothing mattered any more but that he was back and we were in each other's arms again.

Cam remained home for a whole week. During this time we devoted ourselves to the children; Cam painted the summer-house for them and thoroughly enjoyed his unaccustomed do-it-yourself activities.

'I feel like a kid myself,' he told me contentedly as, paint-stained and weary, we proudly surveyed the results of our handiwork.

I think this was the happiest week I'd ever known. The weather was in our favour. We were having an Indian summer. Cam did indeed seem to have shed years and the children all their shyness and reserve. Even Sandra's stammer had suddenly taken a turn for the better, and she had begun to converse much more often and with far less difficulty.

'You're so wonderful for them,' Cam told me. 'I've never seen them so happy.'

Muriel remained, as always, the only fly in the ointment. We did try to include her in our activities but, understandably, I suppose, she said doing up the summer-house was not quite in her line – she preferred to paint pictures.

'Anyway, I want to finish that portrait of you, Kate,' she said with her enigmatic smile, and shut herself away in her studio, only appearing at meal times. Nevertheless, her manner towards me was not unfriendly – as if she, too, had caught something of the gaiety which infected us all. She was, for her, more expansive and certainly much less strict with the children. I felt a bit foolish on several occasions when I tried to explain once again to Cam that I felt Muriel might not be good for the younger ones. Even I was beginning to think that I had misjudged her and that in time I might even grow fond of her.

Cam refused to hear one word against her. 'I just don't know how I'd have managed these last few years without her,' he told me more than once. 'I owe her a great deal, Kate, and so do the children. She's been a real mother to them since Jennifer died.'

No, I thought, not a mother. There was little of the maternal in Muriel. But I did not want to argue the point with Cam. I could see it upset him whenever I tended to speak critically of her.

With each day that passed, I fell a little more deeply in love with my husband. When Joanne wrote to me from London asking at the end of her letter if I had any regrets, I was able to reply perfectly truthfully, 'None, none, none!' I was happier than I'd ever been before.

There were, of course, the very rare occasions when Cam and I did not see eye to eye. I wanted to invite Robert Carnes to dinner one evening, and Cam simply refused to agree. He wouldn't give me a reason, except to say that he couldn't see any point in making the doctor–patient relationship a social one.

Surprisingly, Muriel came into this conversation on my side. 'But Kate likes him, Father, and another male would even out the predominantly female element, wouldn't it?'

Cam was annoyed. I knew it by the quick flush that rose to his cheeks and by the set of his mouth. 'I don't need your advice, thank you, Muriel. I don't want Carnes here as a guest, and that's all there is to it.'

I didn't really care whether Robert came or not. It was true I liked him, but I was perfectly happy just to be alone with the family. But I was piqued by Cam's unreasonableness. He might have considered my wishes – or at least treated my suggestion with a less dogmatic refusal.

Strangely, it was Muriel who put matters right. In a moment when we were alone she said, 'I don't think Father meant to be unreasonable, Kate. I expect he's just a bit jealous.'

'Jealous?' I was too surprised to consider that it was really none of Muriel's business; I had not invited her opinion.

'Well, of course he's jealous!' Muriel repeated in a matter-of-fact voice. 'Dr Carnes is very attractive – and much more your age than Father.'

'That's just stupid, Muriel.' I was angry now. But thinking about it afterwards, I realised that she could well be right. Cam did have a chip on his shoulder about our age difference – something I never thought about myself. Again and again, usually as a prelude to our lovemaking, he would say wistfully, 'I can't think why you should ever have fallen in love with someone my age.'

I always laughed about it and told him I hadn't fallen in love with a man his age but with him. He wasn't old to me but he didn't seem able to forget that he was twice a widower and fourteen years my senior.

He and I were returning to town together on Sunday night. He wanted to spend the following week at his office and was determined not to be parted from me again. Nor did I wish us to be separated, and despite the appeals of the children that I should stay with them, I hardened my heart and told them firmly they must be unselfish. It wasn't for long – we would be back the following Friday evening for the weekend, I said, and laughed at their downcast faces.

I was packed and ready to go by lunch time on Sunday when fate intervened. Mrs Meadows slipped on the back doorstep and broke her arm. I went with her as Cam drove carefully the fifteen miles to the nearest hospital where her arm was X-rayed and the fracture set. Cam and I both assumed she would be admitted to a ward, but there was no question of the hospital taking her in. The wards were full, and she did not need nursing. As the nurse explained, apart from being unable to use her right arm, Mrs Meadows was perfectly fit to go home.

Cam and I discussed the situation while we were in the waiting room. It was obvious Mrs Meadows would be unable to work. It was also obvious that we could not expect Muriel to manage the house, cooking, and children single-handedly.

'I'll just have to stay behind and look after them, darling.' I said miserably.

Cam looked at me with something like desperation. 'But Kate, I can't stay. I have to go to London. I've been away too long as it is, and I don't want to go without you.'

He sounded so like a small boy being packed off against his will to boarding school that I felt even more unhappy. Yet I knew – and Cam did, too – that there was no alternative.

'Perhaps if we could get a girl in from the village, Muriel would...' he began.

But he didn't finish the sentence. It was already five o'clock. There was no time to arrange for someone to come up daily from the village. It would be six o'clock before we were home and even by fast train, Cam would not be in London before midnight.

'Damn, blast, and hell!' Cam said under his breath. He looked furious and miserable.

I held his hand. 'Maybe I can fix something up tomorrow or the next day,' I said. 'Then I'll join you for the last half of the week.'

But I didn't hold out much hope. A new maid would need several days to find her way around the big house before she could be of much help. And there was the cooking. Old Meadows would want feeding, too, and Mrs

Meadows – seven of us for meals. It just wasn't fair to Muriel.

Between getting Mrs Meadows to bed, coping with the children's questions and trying to reassure old Meadows, I barely saw Cam until he called upstairs to me that he was just off. A great wave of misery engulfed me. It was stupid, I know, when we were only saying good-bye for a few days, but we clung to each other in the darkness of the drive as if we were parting for several weeks.

'I love you, I love you,' he kept saying between kisses.

I felt like crying. Matters were not made any better when Muriel suddenly appeared on the front doorstep and said, 'Dr Carnes has just been on the phone. He's heard about Mrs Meadows and says he'll call round after supper and take a look at her.'

I felt Cam stiffen. 'I shouldn't have thought that was necessary,' he said coldly.

My heart sank, but I said brightly. 'Perhaps she'll need something to help her sleep. She is in some pain, darling. Anyway, don't worry about anything – anything at all. I love you,' I added in a whisper that could not reach Muriel's ears.

Cam drove off, frowning and unhappy. I joined Muriel on the doorstep. She was looking at me, her own face expressionless. 'Perhaps I was a little tactless,' she said softly. 'I'd forgotten Father was so jealous of Dr Carnes. I should have waited to mention his visit until after Father had left.'

'Don't be so stupid, Muriel,' I said with a great deal more sharpness than I'd intended. I was, in fact, furious with her although I knew it was unreasonable of me. But it entered my mind that her lack of tact had been deliberate. She could so easily have waited until Cam had gone.

'I'm very sorry, Kate. I didn't think.'

I drew a deep breath and calmed down. With an effort, I put out a hand and patted Muriel's arm. 'It isn't important. Let's not make a fuss about this.'

I withdrew my hand. No matter what Muriel said, it seemed to aggravate me. I must control myself better.

I told her to set the table for supper and went to the kitchen to make omelettes and a salad. There wasn't time to do anything more elaborate.

Old Meadows was sitting in a basket chair smoking a pipe. He broke into a flow of Yorkshire dialect as I came into the room. I shook my head and spread my hands to indicate that I didn't understand much of what he said. Poor old man! It was obvious he was worried that his wife had been put to bed in Quarry House and not in their own cottage. I told him to eat in the kitchen this evening and that Dr Carnes would be along later. He would be able to persuade the old man that it would be better for Mrs Meadows to sleep in the house for a night or two until she felt better. Then she could return to their cottage and both of them could eat there.

One way and another, my customary calmness had given way to a state of nervous tension by the time the doctor arrived. He took one look at my pale taut face and said, 'Looks to me as if you are the one most in need of my attention.'

I had not realised how strung up I was. I'd been badly shaken when I'd found Mrs Meadows groaning and half-fainting on the back doorstep. Since then, having to control myself in front of the children and the emotional upheaval with Cam had taken their toll. I burst into tears.

Robert sat me down in an armchair and while I sniffed into a handkerchief, he went to the sideboard and poured me a brandy.

'Shock!' he said briefly as he pushed it into my hand and stood over me while I drank it.

I felt very foolish once I began to recover my equilibrium. I apologised. Robert smiled.

'You women are all the same. You feel guilty if you give way, yet it's the best possible thing for you, medically speaking. Now tell me what's been going on, before I go up to see Mrs Meadows.'

Suddenly all my tension vanished. Robert's calm sympathetic manner was exactly what I needed, together with the chance to unburden everything onto his shoulders. He listened quietly, his brown eyes warm and understanding. I didn't mean to mention it, but I even blurted out my irritation with Muriel, although I didn't tell him how she had annoyed me. I told him how ashamed I felt at giving way like this over nothing.

'You've no cause whatever to be ashamed of a few tears,' he said. 'You've been under a strain for some time. First, there was the excitement and tension of getting married. Then your honeymoon. Contrary to belief, honeymoons aren't always as therapeutic as one might suppose. It's a strain suddenly having to share yourself with another human being.'

I was surprised. I hadn't thought of my honeymoon as anything but a glorious holiday. Now I realised that Robert was perfectly correct – it was a strain learning to share yourself with another human being. I was used to being alone and although I loved Cam passionately and everything had been quite perfect for both of us, I'd nevertheless had moments of wishing I had just an hour or two of privacy – time to recharge my batteries, calm myself down.

I felt immensely soothed by Robert's philosophy and grateful that at least someone understood me even better than I understood myself.

'You must have second sight!' I told him with a watery smile.

His laughter was frank and spontaneous. 'No such thing. I'm just interested in psychology. Now how about letting me give you a sleeping pill? I'm going to give a knockout dose to Mrs Meadows so she should sleep the night through, and there's no reason why you shouldn't do the same. A good night's rest and you'll feel able to cope with life again tomorrow.'

I nodded. It was rather nice to be told what to do. The responsibilities had all seemed mine up to now. I was happy to allow someone else to give me orders.

It was almost nine o'clock. I asked Robert if he often turned out so late to see his patients of his own free will.

He shook his head. 'You overestimate me. I never turn out unless I have to answer an emergency. I'm busy enough without making unnecessary calls.'

'Then why did you do so for this family?' I asked curiously. I was a little disappointed. When I thought about him at all, I supposed him to be a dedicated man, warm-hearted, personally involved in the welfare of his patients. Now it looked as if we at Quarry House got preferential treatment because we were private patients. Money made the difference.

He was frowning, as if he had not understood me. 'I came here this evening because you asked me to,' he said.

Now I was the one confused. '*I* asked you to?' I repeated. 'But I didn't, Robert!'

'I took the call myself,' Robert said bluntly. 'Muriel told me Mrs Meadows had broken her arm, that you and your husband had taken her to hospital and would like me to look in later to see that all was well.'

My mouth fell open. '*Muriel*...phoned *you*? She told me *you* phoned *her*?'

'But how could I have known Mrs Meadows had broken her arm if someone hadn't told me first?' Robert argued reasonably. I thought about it.

'I suppose I assumed word had gone round the village – or the hospital notified you. I didn't think about it.'

'Is it important?' Robert asked.

I shook my head. 'No, I suppose not. It's just – well, odd! Why should Muriel take it on herself to telephone you and then say you had been the one to make the call?'

Robert shrugged his shoulders.

'Whatever the reason, I think she acted wisely. Even if Mrs Meadows is okay, *you* certainly needed me.'

He was smiling again and, with an effort, I smiled too.

'I expect she guessed you were at the end of your tether,' he said. 'Anyway, I'm glad she did call me.'

So was I. But after Robert had gone, I kept wondering if his was the correct explanation. Had Muriel more sensitivity to my feelings than I had given her credit for? Had she acted in my interest? And, if so, why had she lied about that phone call? Questions chased round my mind like squirrels in a cage.

I thought of broaching the subject openly to her but put off doing so until the morning. I decided to follow Robert's instructions – go to bed and take the sleeping pill he'd given me. No doubt it was all quite unimportant. Perhaps Muriel had not lied, and I had simply heard her incorrectly.

But when I lay on my pillow, dazed and a little befuddled by the drug as it began to do its work, the thought suddenly struck me with cold clarity. Muriel had lied quite deliberately, because she had hoped to and succeeded in – making Cam jealous.

I slept soundly and without dreaming, but I awoke with that ugly suspicion still on my mind, dampening my spirits and casting a horrid shadow on the beginning of a new day.

Chapter Six

Perhaps it was weakness on my part, but I never did pluck up courage to tackle Muriel outright about the telephone call. I talked myself round to the idea that I must have been mistaken about her remark outside on the drive. To give her the benefit of the doubt was the least I could do, more especially as I knew in my heart that I did not like her and therefore had an even greater obligation to try to be fair to her.

Nor did I mention the matter to Cam. It would only add to his worries. He telephoned next evening from London to tell me how much he missed me and to inquire after Mrs Meadows. He sounded so depressed that I didn't even tell him Robert had called again the following day.

After replacing the receiver, I wished I had told him. To omit Robert's name was tantamount to admitting that Cam had cause for jealousy. This was ridiculous. I could not understand why I hadn't spoken out as easily and spontaneously as I would on any other subject. Robert was an attractive man and I liked him, but there was no earthly reason why I shouldn't admit it since I had no room in my heart for anyone but Cam.

I resolved to have it out in the open with Cam next weekend. Nothing was ever made better by pretending it did not exist. If Cam were jealous, I must help him overcome it by letting him see he could trust me absolutely, even in the company of a handsome younger man such as Robert.

Because my conscience was completely clear, I had no hesitation in inviting Robert to stay for a glass of sherry when he called to see Mrs Meadows on the following day. He had been held up by the birth of two babies that morning and so arrived late at Quarry House.

We sat enjoying a drink and the easy conversation that always seemed to flow between us. He told me about the infants he had brought into the world that morning; one an easy birth, the other a breech which had taxed his energy and skill.

'You must be tired now!' I said sympathetically.

'I suppose so. But when it all ends well, the feeling of elation carries you through the rest of the day,' he said. 'It's one of the times I love my job – when I know that I have been instrumental in saving a life. The mother gave up trying after a while, poor soul. Not that I blamed her. She has had a difficult life. The husband knocks her about, I'm afraid.'

'But why?' I asked. 'What makes a man brutal to his wife?'

Robert shrugged. 'Oh, lots of things – frustration, drink, jealousy, fear – more rarely, sadism.'

I fastened on that word 'jealousy'. We discussed its causes and effects. Robert believed it generally sprang from a sense of insecurity. 'A man totally sure of his own worth doesn't suffer from feelings of inadequacy,' he explained. 'Therefore he doesn't fear competition.'

I thought about Cam. Perhaps he felt insecure. He had this silly obsession about his age. Yet, at thirty-eight, he was in his prime, and it seemed so unreasonable for him to doubt that I loved him fully as much as he loved me.

'It's usually very hard for the other partner to accept,' went on Robert, as if he had read my thoughts. 'A man might well not be able to explain the cause of his emotion. Pride, for example, might make him reluctant to admit even to his doctor that he was afraid he might be impotent, or become so. He may know himself a weak character and secretly envy other men's strength. Once one knows his fears, one can explain the jealousy, which is really fear of failing to meet the challenge of competition. In its extreme form, it can become a mental disorder and certainly needs psychiatric treatment. It causes great distress to the recipient, sometimes even turning love to hate. It happened to me once.'

It was then he told me about Cathy, the girl he'd once loved and hoped to marry when he became a qualified doctor. But she had been insanely jealous, creating impossible scenes over any other woman in his life.

'Obviously I was in daily touch with dozens of women,' Robert said. 'Nurses, for the most part. Cathy saw each and every one as a potential rival. At first, I was flattered. I rather enjoyed her possessiveness, but it became worse and worse until I felt I was being strangled. There were one or two embarrassing scenes at the hospital where I was training, and my work began to suffer. Poor Cathy suffered too, but there was nothing I could do about it. I loved her and was entirely faithful to her in thought and deed, but it wasn't enough. Marriage wouldn't have been enough, either. I think the only way she could have been totally convinced I was hers was if she had been able to incarcerate me, like an unborn child, into her womb. In the end I broke off the engagement.'

He paused, his eyes filled with sadness or regret – I could not be sure which.

'Later Cathy had a breakdown,' Robert went on, his voice now toneless. 'She never fully recovered.'

'I'm sorry,' I said.

He gave a slight shrug of his shoulders. 'That's life, Kate. I'm not so silly as to blame myself any more – though I did at the time. I realise now that her nature was unstable and that the breakdown would probably have happened anyway. But I was instrumental in precipitating it, and I loved her. She loved me, too. That was the tragedy.'

'Will she ever get better?'

'Perhaps. She lives at home now with her parents and leads a more or less normal life. But we'll never meet again. The doctor concerned told me that if we were ever to meet, it could send her back into darkness.'

I remained silent. There was nothing I could say to show my sympathy. I wondered how such a situation could have left him so free of bitterness. I'm sure if it had happened to me, I would have felt that life had cheated me cruelly and resented it.

I felt the smallest shiver of fear go through me. I pushed it away quickly. It was absurd to liken Robert's Cathy to my darling Cam. Cam's jealousy was the perfectly normal reaction of any man of his age in love with a young wife.

'You'll meet someone else one day, Robert,' I said lightly, hoping to remove the sadness still lingering on his face. 'In fact, I'm surprised you haven't already done so.'

Robert smiled. 'Too busy,' he replied, matching my tone. 'Besides, someone has always grabbed the attractive girls before I get on the scene.'

'I'm sorry. I didn't mean to interrupt.'

I swung round and saw Muriel standing in the open doorway, looking at us with a strange enigmatic expression.

'Of course you are not interrupting,' I said irritably. And then with an effort, added, 'Come and sit down and have a glass of sherry.'

Muriel remained perfectly still. 'I came to tell you Father is on the phone. He wants to talk to you.'

'Well, why didn't you say so at once!' I cried, jumping up. I felt so angry with Muriel that I wanted to hit her. Robert said, 'I was just going anyway, Kate. Muriel will show me out. I'll see you in a couple of days.'

I nodded and ran out to the hall where the phone lay off its hook. 'Darling! It's me, Kate.' I said.

There was no answering endearment. Cam's voice was icy cold, sarcastic, as he said, 'I gather I've chosen an inconvenient moment to ring.'

'How can you say that!' I protested. 'I always want to talk to you, and you know it.'

'I understood from Muriel you were entertaining your young doctor.'

Colour flooded my cheeks. 'We were having a sherry, darling. He's just left. How are you? Do you miss me?'

The sarcasm in Cam's voice was unmistakable now as he replied, 'Obviously a great deal more than you miss me. I rang to inquire after Mrs Meadows.'

For a few moments we talked of domestic affairs, but I sensed Cam wasn't really paying attention to my news.

'Darling, I can't wait until Friday,' I told him. 'How's work? Are you busy? Do you love me?'

Now at last his voice was softer, warmer. 'You know damn well I do, Kate. I refuse to come away without you again. I don't care if Mrs Meadows breaks her neck. Next time you're coming to London with me, understand?'

I relaxed, not realising until then how tautly I had been holding myself.

'That goes for me, too. I miss you all the time.'

'Do you?' Now there was a wistfulness in Cam's tone that disturbed me afresh. I was hurt that he could doubt it.

'You *know* I do!'

'You seem to be making out all right without me.'

'Cam!' Again that shiver of apprehension went through me. 'It's silly to talk like that. Please don't.'

The line went silent. For a moment, I wondered if we had been cut off. Then Cam said, 'I'll ring you same time tomorrow. Take care of yourself, darling. I love you. Life is meaningless without you.'

He rang off before I could tell him I loved him, before I could even say goodbye.

I felt hurt, bewildered, disappointed and uneasy. Most of all, I think I felt angry.

'Everything all right, Kate?'

Once again Muriel startled me. She seemed to have a way of appearing suddenly beside me, materialising out of thin air. No wonder the children were afraid of ghosts!

'Of course it is,' I said sharply. 'And while you're here, Muriel, exactly what did you say to Cam before you called me to the phone?'

I had not known I was going to ask such a direct question. The words came from me in a long angry rush.

'Why, nothing – nothing at all!' Muriel's face was white in the dark gloom of the hall. 'What did you think I'd said to Father, Kate? Are you sure there is nothing wrong?'

I turned on my heel and walked quickly away up the stairs to my bedroom. I sat down on the edge of the bed and clasped my hands together. They were trembling. I tried to calm down, to stop the ridiculous thoughts that were whirring through my head.

I'm being unfair to Muriel, I told myself sharply. I'm assuming she's trying to make trouble between Cam and me. But what possible reason could she have? I reminded myself that if one once started suspecting a person, there was no end to the number of suspicious interpretations one could put on the most harmless words and actions.

But I could not forget the way Muriel had stood in the drawing-room doorway, looking at Robert and me with that half-smile on her lips; nor forget the cool voice saying: *'I'm sorry, I didn't mean to interrupt!'* inferring that she was breaking in on an intimate little tête-à-tête between Robert and me.

I drew a deep breath. This was quite ridiculous. I must stop thinking this way. Muriel had no reason whatever to wish me harm. I'd done my utmost to befriend her, to make life easier for her ever since I'd arrived at Quarry House. It wasn't even as if Cam were her real father and that she had cause to resent his marriage to me. On the contrary, a new wife who could take over some of the arduous duties that had fallen on her shoulders must surely be a welcome help.

I felt I must be misjudging her. Her strange reticence and reserve had made it hard for me to get close to her. Because she was my only failure so far with the members of Cam's family, I could be trying subconsciously to excuse my own failure by making her out to be some kind of fiend.

So I reasoned with myself and almost succeeded in convincing myself that I was the unbalanced one, that I must get a grip on myself and my imagination.

On a sudden impulse, I went along to Mrs Meadows' room. We had settled her comfortably in the guest room with old Meadows in the dressing room adjoining. She was still in bed, though Robert had said she could get up tomorrow. She was suffering now only from shock, and she herself reassured me that she was in no pain, though a bit uncomfortable.

I sat down by her bed and managed without much difficulty to bring the conversation round to the past.

'You and Meadows have had the gardener's cottage for years, haven't you?' I said. 'So you must know more than anybody about the family. Please tell me about them, Mrs Meadows. My husband doesn't care to talk much about the past ten years or so, and I would like to know.'

'The past wasn't easy for him, poor man,' Mrs Meadows said, happy to have an opportunity to gossip. I felt guilty in encouraging her to do so, but my desire to understand what was happening in Quarry House and to Cam and me was stronger than my principles. 'Small wonder he doesn't care to remember. Not that I was working in the house in those days, mind you. They had live-in staff when Mr Campbell came home with his first bride – Miss Muriel's mother, that was.'

'What was she like?' I asked curiously.

'I never saw her but twice,' Mrs Meadows told me, her face bent over the daily newspaper she held in her hand. 'As I recall, she had much the same looks as Miss Muriel. Older than Mr Campbell, though – kept herself to herself and she seldom went near the village. The maids as was here didn't like her very well – too much the grand lady with them she was. Here in Yorkshire, it doesn't do to be looking down on folks as is working for you.'

I listened, intrigued by what I was hearing.

'Mind you, she was a house-proud woman and kept the place beautiful. Meadows tells me there were always flowers wanted for the house, and she used to call him every morning to tell him what she wanted cut for the vases.'

Mrs Meadows' face darkened as she continued, 'What shocked everyone was when the poor woman fell to her death. Mr Campbell was away on business at the time, and it was only by chance they found her. Old Mr Winter was out riding on the moors and came upon her body, poor soul. She could have lain there for days and no one know better. It was November time, and the mists were down over the moors. I recall Meadows telling me how old Mr Winter came like a ghost himself carrying her body home on the back of his horse – a great white creature it was, clip-clopping towards him in the mist with Mr Winter plodding alongside trying to keep the poor mutilated body from toppling off the horse. Fair shook him up for days, it did. He'd dream about it nights.'

'Poor Meadows!' I could well imagine how unnerved anyone would be by this. The mere thought of it made me shiver.

'And all the time, little Miss Muriel standing at the nursery window a-looking as they brought her mother's body home.'

I caught my breath. No wonder the child had grown up as she was. The shock to her must have been terrible. She could have been only five or six years old at the time.

'Mr Campbell near went off his head. I went to the funeral with Meadows, and I saw Mr Campbell with my own eyes shaking like an aspen tree and trembling all the while. He went back to London after the funeral. Best thing for him, I said at the time. He didn't come back till Mrs Grant gave up minding the child – Miss Muriel that is. Then he came down from London with the new nanny.'

'Jennifer!' I said under my breath.

The old woman nodded.

'Now there was a lady everyone liked!' Mrs Meadows said, putting down her paper. 'A vicar's daughter she was, and brought up to charitable ways. She always had time for the village folk, and she was that patient with Miss Muriel. Gone a bit wild, Meadows told me, but Mrs Jennifer gentled her the way you might handle a spirited pony.'

'And Mr Rivers?' I asked. 'Was he happy?'

'Indeed he was. Most of the staff had been given notice when the house was shut up, so when he brought his second wife home, he asked me to come in as daily cook. Not that Mrs Jennifer couldn't cook very well herself, but it wasn't long before the first baby was on the way and she couldn't manage by herself, so I came to the cottage to live in. Next thing, so it seemed, the house was full of babies.

Mrs Jennifer was a good mother to them all, and things were settling down very happily when...'

She broke off as if she could not bring herself to talk about the second tragedy.

'It must have been terrible for everyone,' I said softly.

The old woman sighed. 'Village folk did say then that Quarry House was haunted by an evil spirit!' she said. 'Not that I hold with such superstitious nonsense, but you can understand why they said so. There was only me and Mr Meadows as would work here and take care of the children. Mr Campbell was completely broken up. They do say that he looked like a ghost himself at the inquest. Meadows was there. He'd been the one to discover poor Mrs Jennifer's body, so he had to witness. Of course, the verdict was accidental death, but in the village they said it was foul play.'

Her words shook me.

'But there was never any doubt, surely?' I asked.

'It was doctor's evidence cast the doubt. Seems he couldn't understand how Mrs Jennifer could have injured her head so badly when she fell,' Mrs Meadows said. 'Mr Campbell's lawyer pointed out that the rocks below the water in the lake could have caused the injuries but the doctor – old Dr Williams, that was – he kept on saying he didn't think so. But everyone knew him as a stubborn old man, and there being no one who could possibly have wanted to harm Mrs Jennifer, it stood to reason it was an accident. Leastways, no one had any evidence to say otherwise and that's how the verdict stood.'

'Poor Cam!' I said. 'How awful for him.'

Mrs Meadows gave me a long, kindly look.

'We said as how we thought he never would marry again,' she told me. 'My heart bled for those poor little children and though Meadows was against it, I felt it was my duty to stay and care for them. It was God's will, I told him, and he'd just have to accept it same as myself.'

'I think it was very good of you, Mrs Meadows.'

'All the same, they needed a real mother,' she said with the deep conviction of a woman who knows her place in the world. 'Self-educated I am, and that's not fitting for young ladies, though I do know how a young girl should behave even though I'm lowly born. I knew the ways Mrs Jennifer taught them, and I just went on the same. But I was that pleased when I heard Mr Campbell was marrying again, thought I did wonder with you being so young...'

'I know,' I broke in, laughing. 'You wondered if I'd turn out to be a flibbertigibbet!'

She laughed with me. We were now firm friends.

'Meadows says he feels better now I've broken my arm,' she told me confidentially. 'That's the third accident, he said, so we've had our run of bad luck complete and no harm will come to you.'

'Harm? To me?'

'Bad luck goes in threes,' Mrs Meadows said, sighing. 'So the devil's had his due and God can have his way in this house again.'

I was at a loss for words. The old woman's strange mixture of superstition and religion confused me.

I thought once more about Muriel's childhood – so very much worse than my own. It was a wonder she had grown up as normal as she was under the circumstances. The second death must have revived all her memories of her mother's accident, and no doubt she was old enough when Jennifer died to hear of and understand the rumours that were rife after the inquest.

'Mark my words, Mr Campbell is right – the past is best forgotten,' Mrs Meadows said. 'It's over and done, Mrs Kate, and not for you to worry about.'

She was right, of course. But I felt better for having talked to her. I hadn't learned much that was new, but at least the conversation had revived all my earlier intentions to be kinder and more loving towards Muriel. There were so many grim reasons why she should be unusual.

But as for Quarry House being haunted, that was nonsense. I put the thought out of my mind. I wanted to concentrate on Cam, Mrs Meadows' account of the past had given me a greater understanding of him. No wonder, after losing happiness twice, he was so possessive with me. Deep down in his mind, he must feel that fate was against him and might find some terrible way to take me from him.

'It's my sudden unaccountable death he should worry about,' I told myself with a smile. 'Not my perfectly harmless friendship with poor Robert.'

As I peeled potatoes, I pondered the question of my growing friendship with the young doctor. If it would make Cam happier, I would bring it to an end. Yet reason told me not to do this. No one ever conquered a fear by running away from it. I wanted to go on seeing Robert, to get to know him better and to have Cam get to know and like him. If we could only achieve the first few steps, Cam would see how little he had to fear. Robert would be the first friend we had made together.

But even as the thought passed through my mind, I knew in my heart that it wasn't going to work...not unless I could convince Cam that Robert was virtually unimportant in my life. This I might find hard to do since in a way I could not myself understand, I knew that I needed Robert badly, not just as our family doctor but as my friend.

Chapter Seven

Two days later I had my first chance to try to establish a new rapport with Muriel. Mrs Meadows was up and about again, and although she could not do anything much in the house, she told me she was quite well able to sit with the younger girls in the nursery and keep them amused. The weather had changed again and it was pouring so heavily that any outdoor activity was out of the question.

So, with a free afternoon on my hands, I invited Muriel to join me in the drawing-room. 'I thought I'd light the fire to be more cheerful,' I told her, 'but of course, I'll understand if you have something else you'd rather do?'

Her face, so often expressionless, held now a look of surprise. 'I've nothing much I must do,' she said slowly and a little ungraciously.

'Then do come and keep me company. I'm about to attack a full basket of mending for the children. The time will pass much more quickly if there is someone to talk to.'

I suppose we both realised that I could have gone up to the nursery if I was lonely and done my work there. However, Muriel just nodded her head and said, 'I'll help you if you like.'

I felt curiously elated. Perhaps this was the first crack in the ice.

I need not have worried as to how to start the conversational ball rolling. To my surprise, Muriel began to talk as soon as were settled on the sofa in front of the fire with our sewing.

'If this is not too personal a subject, Kate, I still don't understand *why* you married Father.'

Muriel's head was bent over her work. She was sewing a button on one of Lillian's shirts and seemed absorbed in the task.

'He's so much older than you,' she went on. 'Doesn't that worry you?'

'Why should it? There is fourteen years' difference, but I don't see that age matters when you really love someone.'

'I do,' Muriel said, not argumentatively but in a cool matter-of-fact voice. 'In fact, I know it does. Father married my mother, who was eight years older than he. It didn't work.'

'But Muriel, how can you say such a thing?' I burst out impulsively.

She looked up and gave me that curious smile of hers. It held no humour. It was almost patronising – as if she found me gauche, her inferior.

'Mother left a diary. It proves she was very unhappy with Father.'

Muriel's voice was matter-of-fact. I found her statement embarrassing and would have dropped the subject, but for the fact that Muriel obviously wished to continue. 'The diary makes interesting reading,' she said tonelessly.

I felt the need to caution her. 'I don't think you should read someone else's private thoughts,' I said. 'Your mother can't have wanted you to look at her diary.'

'Then she should have put it somewhere where I wasn't likely to find it,' Muriel answered quietly. 'Instead, she locked it up in her dressing-table drawer with a note saying that in the event of her death, I was to keep it and read it on my twelfth birthday.'

I was so surprised I couldn't think of an immediate reply. Silence hung between us, broken only by the faint crackle of the burning logs in the grate.

'I don't think you should allow yourself to dwell too much on the past, Muriel,' I said at last, finding my voice. 'It can't make anything better and it will only depress you.'

Muriel returned to her sewing. 'Perhaps not. But it's only natural I should go on thinking about it,' she said softly. 'After all, you wouldn't forget it if your mother had been forced to kill herself, would you?'

I gasped. If Muriel's intention had been to shock me, she had certainly succeeded.

I tried to remain calm. 'That is a terrible thing to say, Muriel, and I'm quite certain it isn't true. Even if she were as unhappy as you say, she would never have reacted as you suggest. She was your mother. She wouldn't have left you alone in the world. Her death was a tragic accident, not suicide.'

'I've often tried to believe that,' Muriel shrugged. 'I can quite understand *your* wishing to do so. After all, you're the wife of the man who drove her to her death. You wouldn't care to think of Father as a murderer.'

Now at last I really was speechless. Anger, shock, distress, all held me in a cold grip. I was sure now that Muriel was a little mentally deranged. She could not say such things if she were sane.

'I suppose I've shocked you,' she broke the silence. 'I forgot for the moment that you loved Father – or think you do. If you knew...'

'Muriel, I won't listen to any more of this,' I broke in. 'I'm trying not to be angry because I realise you've been under a great strain for many years. You were only a little girl when this terrible thing happened, and facts can become distorted in a child's eyes. So I'm not angry, but I am absolutely sure that you ought to get away from this house – at least, for a while. Have you ever considered going to a good art school? You have such talent – it seems a great shame to waste it.'

Instead of replying to my question directly, she said, 'It's funny, but you remind me so much of Jennifer. You and she have a lot in common. You share that remarkable quality – innocence.'

Somehow, her words restored my sense of proportion. It even had its funny side – this eighteen-year-old sitting in judgment as if she were the adult and I the child. She sounded almost sorry for me!

Gently, with as much patience and sympathy as I could muster, I told her again that I thought it would be good for her to get away. In fact, I intended to talk to Cam about it and insist that he agreed to her having a flat of her own and no responsibilities, preferably far away from Quarry House.

Muriel looked up once more from her sewing and her face softened into a smile, the first that I had ever seen with real warmth in it.

'It's such a shame,' she said, more to herself than to me. 'You're a kind person, Kate. It would all have been so much easier if I hadn't liked you.'

'What would have been easier?' I asked sharply. I hated her way of talking in riddles.

'I shall mind when you go,' she said, shrugging her shoulders.

'But I am not going anywhere. Where do you mean, go? To London, with Cam?' I was angry again. 'I do wish you'd say what you mean, Muriel.'

The look she now gave me was quite without humour. 'If I did say what I mean, you'd never believe me. I'm only trying to warn you, Kate – albeit in a roundabout way –

that you aren't safe here at Quarry House. I can see from your face that already you're doubting me, so I'm just wasting my breath. But you've tried to be kind to me and the girls love you – that's why I wanted to warn you. But it's no use, is it? You aren't going to listen to me.'

'Most certainly not,' I cried. 'If you want to frighten me, Muriel, you'll have to be a lot more specific. I'd like to know, for instance, just *what* you are warning me about? Or is it *someone*? Or could it be that you are jealous because I am happy and you are not? Is that it, Muriel? Are you trying to make me unhappy? Insecure?'

The faint look of pity which crossed her face made me wish the unguarded words unspoken. Whatever crazy idea she had in her mind, I didn't really feel she had any personal antipathy towards me. But I wasn't going to listen to any more of such nonsense and I told her so. 'If you can't be more specific, then kindly don't talk this way again,' I told her.

'I'm sorry, Kate,' she sighed. 'But Logan agreed I ought to warn you.'

'Logan? What has he to do with all this? You've no right to discuss me with anyone else, Muriel.'

'But I've no one else to advise me,' Muriel came back with a compelling simplicity. 'Certainly not Father, not the girls, not poor Mrs Meadows, who'd run away like a frightened rabbit and never be seen again. So you see, Kate, I have to talk to Logan.'

'Are you in love with him?'

I don't know what prompted my question. There was no hesitation before Muriel's reply. 'I don't think I know what love is. I know, of course, what it is supposed to be but I don't seem capable of loving the way other girls do – blindly. My eyes have been opened, and I'm doomed to see people as they are – not as I'd like them to be.'

An artist's eye, I wondered as I listened curiously to the girl in spite of my newly aroused antipathy to her? Or was she just prejudiced by life? Did she believe the awful things she professed to believe? If she really thought Cam had been even indirectly responsible for her mother's death, why had she stayed here, looking after his house, his children, him? She had accused him of driving her mother to suicide. Nothing made sense.

I had said I did not intend to discuss the subject further, but despite this, I pressed her now to tell me why she stayed at Quarry House.

'Oh, for a number of reasons. At first, there were the children. I couldn't leave them really, could I? Besides, I was only twelve when I read Mother's diary. This was my home, and I'd always looked on Cam as my father. It took me some time to believe my mother's words. Then there was Jennifer. I liked her and I thought I could protect her. I failed, of course, but I was very young. I couldn't foresee how it would all work out. Anyway, Kate, where could I have gone? I had no money, no home, no relations to go to.'

I felt hopelessly confused. From what had Muriel hoped to protect Jennifer? Could she really believe that Cam had driven his first wife to suicide? It was laughable and utterly pathetic. I had little doubt now that Muriel was not normal. I determined that I would talk to Robert about her as soon as possible. It was fortuitous that he was so interested in psychology.

Now I put an end to this whole fantastic conversation by suggesting to Muriel that we have tea. Nothing had been resolved about her going to art school, but there would be time enough for this when I knew if Robert felt she was mentally capable of living her own life and thought it desirable, as I did. For all I knew he, as the family doctor, might already be aware of her mental state; and this could be the reason why she was still living at home.

Muriel went to her studio as soon as nursery tea was over. Mrs Meadows was reading a story to the little girls, so I decided to take the opportunity to drive down to the village to see Robert. Muriel was so much on my mind that I was afraid I would never be able to sleep that night for worrying.

Evening surgery hours were almost over when I arrived. I had only to wait a few minutes before Robert called for the next patient.

'I'm not ill – just in need of advice,' I said as I seated myself at Robert's desk. Quickly, before I could change my mind about telling him so bizarre a story, I related as factually as I could the incredible accusations Muriel had made during our sewing session.

Robert looked astonished and worried. 'Doesn't sound too good, does it?' he said. 'I'm glad you told me, Kate. Of course it's all nonsense.'

I nodded, sighing. 'I suppose her imagination has run away with her, or *is* she mental in some way? What am I going to do about it, Robert? I can't tell Cam.'

Robert gave me a long searching look. 'But you must, Kate. There is no justification for keeping this from him. She is his responsibility. She cannot be permitted at her age to frighten you or anyone else with her morbid fantasies.'

I stared at him aghast. 'But I *couldn't* tell him. He'd be terribly hurt. Don't you understand, Robert, Muriel more or less made him out to be responsible for the deaths of both his wives. She actually used the word "murderer".'

Robert laid a hand on mine soothingly. It was warm, dry, and comforting.

'Perhaps Campbell knows already how Muriel feels, and has kept it from you because he knows how shocked you would be – and are – by such an idea.'

I felt suddenly cold. If Cam *did* already know, then he should have told me, trusted me.

'Help me, Robert! I honestly don't think I can talk to Cam about it. Does he *have* to know? Can't you just see Muriel – treat her?'

'Kate, Muriel is eighteen. I'm her doctor, but I can't force her to come to me or to accept advice or treatment. You must talk to your husband.'

'I'd feel better if I could convince myself Muriel was deliberately inventing all this in order to make trouble between me and Cam, perhaps hoping I'll leave him and she'll be mistress of Quarry House again. But she has no motive for wanting me out of the way. It is only by my being at Quarry House that she has any chance of making a life for herself. I'm her freedom, not her jailer!'

'I wish you weren't involved,' said Robert, more to himself than to me.

I suppose this was the first time I had any inkling that Robert was personally concerned about me. I'm sure those unguarded words slipped out without his realising how much they betrayed. I wanted Robert as my friend – the only friend I knew up here. I liked him very much, and I knew he liked me. I hoped fervently that our relationship could remain totally platonic. But this was not the moment to worry about our friendship. I said firmly, 'Cam, Muriel, and the children are my family now. Of course I must be concerned about them.'

'Yes, of course,' he agreed, his eyes now focused not on me but on his short, square fingers as they toyed with his pen. He had firm, capable hands. 'I don't seem to be able to offer you any constructive advice, other than to reiterate that I think you should confide in your husband,' he went on. 'Perhaps if you would talk more with Muriel – persuade her to come down to me for a checkup. I haven't had occasion to treat her medically. I *will* have a word with old

Dr Williams, just in case he can throw any light on the matter. He knew her well, I believe.'

'But you won't repeat what I told you?' I begged him quickly. I couldn't bear the thought of anyone else knowing the dreadful accusations Muriel had brought against Cam.

'Not if you don't wish it,' he promised.

Afterwards, driving home, I thought over my conversation with Robert and came to the conclusion that I might have made a bit of a fool of myself. I'd taken Muriel's extraordinary ideas far, far too seriously. I should have laughed them off. I was puzzled now why Robert had not done so. It could only mean that he, too, thought it was no laughing matter; that he had the same fear that there was something very wrong with Muriel – something which could even prove dangerous.

I did not understand myself any longer. I was as a rule a logical person, not given to unaccountable fears or suspicions. Now, for no explicable reason, I was floundering out of my depth in a totally irrational way.

Muriel did not appear at supper. I was worried until Sandra told me she'd left a message to say she was working in the studio and did not want to be interrupted.

The children and I ate our spaghetti at the nursery table. I couldn't face the big dining room this evening. I wanted the cosy atmosphere of the schoolroom with its doll's house and games cupboard and worn linoleum floor. The children were in an infectious giggly mood and soon I was laughing and joking with them. My spirits remained high while I supervised their baths, tucked them in bed, and kissed them goodnight. They might have remained so had not little Lillian clung to me, begging me to stay a little longer.

'I'm so frightened,' she whispered in my ear, 'I don't like ghosts.'

I switched on her little bedside lamp and sat with her until she fell asleep. Each of the girls had a bedroom of her own, but I wondered now if it might not be a good idea to put them all together. They were used to big dormitories at school, and it would certainly make Lillian less nervous to sleep with her elder sisters.

I peeped into the other girls' rooms before I went along the passage to my own. It seemed very large and empty without Cam. I turned on the electric fires, as much for the comfort of their cheerful glow as for warmth. I wished desperately that Cam were home beside me.

I had a long hot bath and climbed into bed, determined to concentrate on my book – the last of the Churchill diaries which Cam had made me read and which I was finding quite fascinating.

But tonight the book could not hold my attention. I was in a grasshopper state of mind where my thoughts leaped from one worry to another – Cam, Muriel, Lillian, Robert... I wished now I had asked Robert for another sleeping pill. Usually one of those people who can drop off the moment their heads touch the pillow, I'd never had the slightest need of drugs to help me sleep. Tonight I did, I heard the hall clock chime the hours – eleven, midnight, one, two. I began to feel desperate.

I suppose at last I did fall into an uneasy doze. It cannot have been a deep sleep, for I'm certain that I was instantly awake at the first of the child's piercing screams. I was certain it came from Lillian. I threw back the bedclothes and flung my dressing gown round me. The screams were non-stop and quite hysterical. I ran down the passage and halted outside Lillian's room. The noise was not coming from there although I could hear her whimpering. I paused, turning toward the adjoining room that was Debbie's. I pushed open the door to see her sitting up in bed, hugging her knees, her eyes wide and frightened but tearless.

'It's Sandy,' she whispered. 'It must be her turn to have the dream. We all get it, you know...the same one, I mean.'

But I couldn't stop to listen to her explanation. The screams were reaching a crescendo and I had to stop them. Never again, I vowed, while I lived in this house would I permit a child to be as frightened as this. I couldn't bear it.

Unconsciously I lifted my hands and covered my ears.

Chapter Eight

It was some time before Sandra was calm enough to talk. I held her shuddering little body, wet with sweat, tightly against my own. Debbie had followed me into the room and was leaning up against me as if she, too, needed comfort.

'It's all right, darling,' I said over and over again. 'It was only a dream.'

'But it's so horrid!' Debbie whispered beside me. 'The ghost dream is the worst of the lot.'

'But I promise you, children, there just aren't such things as ghosts. They're just made-up things for story books.'

'N-n-not t-this o-one!' Sandra gulped 'T-this one is r-r-real. It's t-t-the m-m-man who p-pushed M-mummy into...'

Involuntarily I clapped my hand over the child's mouth. 'Sssh!' I commanded fiercely. 'You mustn't ever say such things, Sandy.'

'Yes, we know.' Debbie said. 'We've both promised never to tell anyone, but you're different.'

I sat silent, horrified and not understanding. Two pairs of eyes regarded me solemnly.

'But who on earth told you such a terrible story?' I said, more to myself than to them.

'I did!'

I jumped, every nerve in my body crying out against the unexpectedness of another voice in the room. I turned my head and saw Muriel standing in the doorway in her long white nightdress. She looked like a ghost herself, and at that moment I was as frightened as either of the children.

Fear made me angry. I was so furious I sprang to my feet and started towards Muriel as though I meant to strike her. But I remembered in time the two little girls who had already seen and heard quite enough. I turned back and said, 'Debbie, you jump into bed beside Sandy and keep her company.'

Sandra's tear-stained face and Debbie's little white face changed with the abruptness of childhood into wreaths of smiles.

'You mean we can sleep together – all night?'

I nodded. 'But no talking,' I added, trying to sound as normal as possible.

Muriel had backed into the passage and stood there waiting for me to leave the room. She was perfectly calm. 'I expect you want an explanation,' she said. 'Shall we go to my room or yours?'

I calmed myself with the memory that this girl could in all probability be mentally sick. Anger would achieve nothing. I must try to stay as calm as she was.

'Your room,' I said, and followed her along the landing.

I don't know why I should have expected anything different, but I was struck nonetheless by the complete orderliness of Muriel's bedroom. Her day clothes were folded over the chair. Her dressing table was neat, her belongings tidily arranged.

'Well?' I asked, sitting down on an empty chair. I was afraid my trembling legs would not support me if I remained standing.

Muriel walked past me unhurriedly and stood by the window, one hand holding a fold of the long blue curtains. 'I told the children a man had pushed Jennifer into the lake,' she said conversationally. 'I had to stop them going near the waterfall. It was the best way I could think of.'

'But it's horrible – *horrible!*' I cried. 'Terrifying little girls with such a dreadful idea!'

Muriel looked at me coldly. Again I had the impression that her expression was pitying. 'How else could I have stopped them, Kate? The girls were very young when it all happened. You know what children are like. You tell them not to go somewhere and they go just because it's forbidden.'

I could not follow her reasoning. 'But to let them think that someone deliberately harmed their mother...' I broke off, too appalled to continue.

Muriel let go the curtain and took a step towards me. Involuntarily I stiffened. She must have seen my movement for she halted and said quietly, 'I don't for one moment expect you will believe me, Kate, but what I am telling you is the truth. Someone *did* push Jennifer. That same someone might push any or all of the children into the lake. Now do you understand why I *had* to frighten them into staying away?'

'You're mad!' The words came out before I could stop them. But Muriel seemed quite unmoved by them.

'I was aware you would consider me so, Kate – otherwise I might have told you this the other day. Nonetheless, it is the truth. Better the girls should be frightened by ghosts and nightmares than go innocently to their slaughter the way Jennifer did.'

I was by now completely out of my depth. I was also very, very frightened. Mrs Meadows had gone back to her cottage with her husband, and I was alone in the house with the three little ones and this insane girl. I'd no doubt in my mind now that Muriel was mad. I wondered if I could somehow reach the telephone and ring Robert. But I was afraid lest Muriel, calm for the moment anyway, should become incensed and get violent.

'I don't think we should discuss this any more tonight,' I said. 'I'm sure you believe you acted for the best, Muriel, so don't worry about it now. Go back to bed and try to sleep.'

As I stood up Muriel sighed. 'I knew you wouldn't believe me. Poor Kate!'

I thought she was going to let me leave the room but she swung round and caught my arm in a fierce grip as I stood up to go.

'If you won't take notice of anything else I say, I do beg you, Kate, not to mention this to Father. Promise me that, won't you? Promise me, *for your own sake!*'

Gently, my skin crawling at her touch, I extricated my arm. 'Stop worrying!' I said as soothingly as I could. 'I'm here to look after you all. You've nothing to fear.'

Muriel was still standing in the middle of the room as I reached the door. Once again, I saw that half-smile on her lips – that pitying smile which so unnerved me.

'Poor Kate,' she said again. 'It isn't I who should be afraid. It's you!'

I forced myself to walk along the landing to my own room. Every nerve in my body demanded that I run, but pride forbade it. I had a mental picture of Muriel standing with her ear to the door, listening to see if she had succeeded in terrifying me the way she had the children.

But once I had locked my door behind me, I collapsed on my bed, legs and arms trembling. I wished with every fibre of my being that Cam was here to cope with the situation. I certainly could not. I was so far out of my depth now that I wasn't sure of anything any more. Perhaps I ought to have locked Muriel's door. For all I knew, she might go into the children's rooms, do them some terrible harm. I needed advice desperately.

It was three a.m.; not a time when I could telephone someone for help. But perhaps Cam wouldn't mind being woken so late at night when I explained...

My hand, reaching out for the telephone by my bed, remained poised there. How could I possibly explain all this to Cam on the phone? And how could he help from three hundred miles away in London? Even if he left at once to drive home, he couldn't be here in the house with me before morning.

'Oh, God, help me!' I prayed aloud without realising I was doing so. Then my eyes went to the slip of paper lying on the bed table. It was the page Robert had torn from his prescription pad as he jotted down his telephone number, saying, 'If I'm not in the office, this number will always find me. Don't hesitate to ring me if ever you need anything.'

Little did I think then that I was going to need help so soon, if ever! Robert was used to being awakened in the middle of the night, called out for emergencies. He would understand. He would tell me what to do.

I must have been in such a panic that even now I can't remember what I did between dialling his number and going down to the kitchen to unlock the back door to let him in. I had only expected him to advise me what to do over the telephone, but he insisted on coming in person to Quarry House. I know the time seemed interminable while I waited for him to arrive. Then suddenly he was there, and I was clinging to him half-hysterically and his arms were round me, firm, steadying, wonderfully welcome.

He pushed me into Mrs Meadows' favourite wicker chair and put on the kettle. He refused to allow me to say a word until I had finished at least half a cup of the strong tea he made in the old brown kitchen teapot. Then he sat down at the table and seeing I was calmer, made me tell him once more exactly what had happened.

'You had quite a shock, didn't you?'

My voice trembled as I finished. 'I just didn't know what to do. *Is* Muriel crazy? Or am I?'

'You're going to have to tell Campbell about this no matter how much you dislike the idea,' Robert explained. 'And the sooner the better. What you've told me explains a great deal about the children, anyway. With Muriel spinning them such tales, it's small wonder they're bundles of nerves – Sandra with her stutter, Lillian running temperatures for no reason and Debbie having nightmares.'

'Thank goodness they spend a large part of their lives away from Muriel, from here,' I said. 'I'm amazed, though, that they've never told anyone before.'

'Muriel probably extracted a promise of secrecy under some dire threat of disaster if they told. "The ghost" would get them or something equally horrifying. You should be flattered, Kate, that they trusted you with "the secret".'

'I almost wish they hadn't,' I said, shuddering. 'Of course it can't be true, can it, Robert? Not the ghost, but the man deliberately pushing Jennifer...'

'No, of course not,' Robert broke in sharply.

I don't know how he guessed the thought that next went through my aching head, but he did for he said quietly, 'And I'm sure Muriel didn't push her either. Jennifer fell. It was an accident and that's a fact established at the inquest.'

But however firmly he spoke, I felt he wasn't certain any more than I was. The only thing I was completely sure about was that if anyone did push Jennifer, it certainly had not been Cam.

'You wouldn't like to think of Father as a murderer!'

Muriel's words, spoken about Cam and her own mother, came with horrifying clarity into my mind. Robert, who must have been watching my face, said, 'What's wrong, Kate? You're not feeling sick?'

I held my head between my hands, my head bursting. 'I'm...okay!' I managed.

'I wish I could get you away from this house.'

Robert's words jolted me back to normality. I realised suddenly that we were virtually alone in the house; me only semi-clothed and Cam away. It would certainly provide some gossip for the village if anyone had seen or heard Robert's car drive up. Muriel, I thought, hysterical again. She could make a lovely story out of this for Cam!

Then I came to my senses. Robert was a doctor. It was as a doctor I had called him here.

But as a friend, too, I thought. Because he's a man, and I like and trust him and need his help.

I was so tired that reason deserted me. I couldn't any longer be sure that my motives were any better than the village might impart. Perhaps unintentionally, I had taken advantage of the fact that I knew Robert liked me; that he was glad I'd called him; that I was dependent on him for help.

'I shouldn't have brought you out in the middle of the night,' I muttered stupidly.

'That really is nonsense. You know I wouldn't have had it otherwise. And you certainly shouldn't have to face this kind of thing alone – that's certain. When does Campbell get home?'

'Friday evening.'

'Can't you ask him to come back tomorrow? He should be here to look after you,' Robert said. He sounded angry.

'I'll ring him tomorrow – I mean, this morning.'

'You're to tell him everything!' Robert commanded. 'I want your promise, Kate. *Everything*. Don't try to spare him because you think he might be hurt. He has to know. You understand?'

I nodded. 'Would...would you be here when I do tell him?' The request was out before I had considered it. As I spoke, I knew at once that Cam wouldn't like Robert being involved. He probably wouldn't like the thought that I'd called him out in the middle of the night, either.

'If you want me, I'll come,' Robert said. 'It's your decision, Kate. Whatever you say goes.'

'Well, we'll see,' I retracted. 'I'll phone. And, Robert, what about Muriel – now, I mean? Ought I to have locked her in her room? Do you think the children are safe?'

He hesitated, deliberating the question. When he replied, he sounded perfectly sure of himself. 'No! I expect she's asleep. She hasn't had the shock you've had. Remember, she's had these thoughts in her mind for years. So have the little girls. Nothing that has happened here tonight is a surprise to them. It's my guess everything will be just as usual when you all meet for breakfast.'

I felt suddenly much calmer. Robert's words made sense. 'You're a good doctor, Robert,' I told him, attempting a smile. 'When you do make up your mind, you sound so convincing that I'm sure none of your patients ever doubt your decisions. I feel miles better. I'll go to bed and sleep it off.'

We both stood up. There was a moment of awkwardness while we stood there like two gauche adolescents unable to find the right social formula for good-bye. Then he smiled and said, 'Good idea! I'll see myself off. Goodbye, Kate. I may see you tomorrow.'

He turned and went out through the back door, leaving me standing there staring after him, wondering why all the warmth seemed suddenly to have left the room.

Chapter Nine

I had been married seven weeks. I loved Cam with all my heart, and it hurt me almost physically to be the one to have to hurt him. But I knew Robert was right – I must tell Cam about Muriel and let him make some decision.

I was on tenterhooks all day waiting for his arrival. Muriel, on the other hand, seemed quite unmoved when I told her her stepfather would be home a day earlier than we had expected him. Without any outward sign of concern for herself – and I think she was astute enough to realise I had sent for Cam – she merely repeated last night's warning: 'Don't mention any of this to Cam for your own sake, Kate!'

I ignored her remark.

I sat in my room staring down the long drive watching for Cam's car, needing him in a way I had never needed him before. At last he came.

For the first few minutes when we were together again and alone, he refused to discuss anything while he held me in his arms, kissing me hungrily and telling me over and over again how much he loathed being parted from me.

'I know it's only been a few days, darling, but it has seemed an eternity. I was so happy when you rang this morning. I knew then that you were missing me as much as I've missed you. Darling, darling Kate!'

My heart sank. I had thought it wisest not to try making any explanations on the telephone. He'd jumped to the conclusion that I'd begged him to come home because I loved him. He still had no idea anything was wrong.

We sat down on the edge of the bed, Cam still holding me as if he couldn't bear to let me be even an inch apart from him. His eyes were riveted on my face, hungrily devouring me. He said, 'Do you know, darling, once or twice I have been stupid enough to imagine that you weren't half as much in love with me as I am with you. The thought nearly drove me mad at night when I tried to sleep and couldn't.'

'Oh, Cam!' I cried, not knowing whether to take him seriously or not. 'You *know* I love you. Don't ever doubt me.'

Perhaps I put a little too much emphasis on the last sentence. Cam gave me a quick, searching glance. 'Might I have cause to do so?' He hesitated and added in a low voice, 'You haven't, I hope, been seeing more of that Carnes fellow?'

Goodness knows I was long past the blushing stage but now, to my dismay, I felt my face slowly suffuse with red. I had nothing to feel guilty about, yet to Cam's penetrating eyes I must have looked as though I had. He gripped my arm and said, 'You have had him here again, then?'

I drew my arm away. With a great effort I kept my voice down as I replied, 'Robert has been here twice, Cam – once to see Mrs Meadows and once to see me. Don't look like that, darling. If you will listen, I'll explain why. Actually, it has to do with the reason I wanted you to come home today.'

Slowly, haltingly, I told him everything. Cam's face remained totally expressionless throughout my account. He seemed neither surprised nor shocked. Indeed, he gave no hint of any reaction until I told him that I had felt it necessary to phone Robert. Only then did his mouth tighten and I felt his body stiffen beside me.

'You'd no right to do that. It was totally unnecessary,' he said in a low, hard voice.

'But, darling, I had to have advice. Don't you see, I wasn't sure if Muriel could be dangerous – really dangerous. I couldn't take the responsibility myself. Naturally I...'

I broke off, astounded to hear Cam laughing. It wasn't hysteria – just plain ordinary laughter.

'Stop it,' I cried. 'Stop it, Cam, please! There's nothing in the least funny about all this. To me, it is all quite horrifying.'

The laughter stopped. Cam stood up and looked down at me. 'I can't believe you took Muriel seriously,' he said in a perfectly normal tone of voice. 'You don't honestly think there's any truth in all her nonsense?' He began to smile again.

I jumped up, facing him with a determination that equalled my bewilderment at his unexpected reactions. 'Of course I don't *believe* it, Cam. But if Muriel is capable of believing the shocking things she says, it means she is ill – mentally ill. Moreover, what she says and does is affecting the little ones. Something has to be done.'

Cam continued to stare at me as if I were hysterical. Off guard, I added, 'Robert agrees with me. He says Muriel may well be suffering from delusions and...'

'I'm not interested in Robert's quack ideas!'

I sat down on the bed, stupefied. This couldn't be Cam – my intelligent, mature, wise husband talking like this.

'Frankly, Kate, I'm forced to the conclusion that you've been making a very large mountain out of a very small molehill. I quite fail to understand your motive – unless it was to provide an excuse to get Robert up here in the middle of the night.'

I gasped. For a moment, I wondered if I could believe my ears. Instinctively, I put a hand to my mouth to prevent myself from saying something I would regret: I stared at him incredulously. He looked pale and strained. His fine grey eyes, so warm and charming as a rule, were like stones. His whole expression had changed – hardened.

'You must be mad,' I whispered. 'How can you make such a crude suggestion? You didn't mean it, did you?'

'Oh, yes, I meant it all right!'

He began to walk up and down the room, hands clenched at his side. His body was shaking.

As steadily as I could, I said, 'You had no justification – none at all!'

He swung around to face me and went on speaking in that harsh, cruel voice that I barely recognised.

'You don't seem to realise what you've been doing to me. Ever since we arrived at Quarry House, you've encouraged that damned young doctor of yours to come here – and on the flimsiest of pretexts. I wish to God he'd never taken old Williams' place. Williams was a decent genuine old family physician. Quack or no quack, Robert Carnes is a pompous young ass who throws his weight about and thinks he can tell me what to do and come up here whenever he damned well likes.' Cam stopped, coughing, swallowing.

I, too, was shaking now from head to foot and I interrupted, shouting at him, 'I've never heard such nonsense. There's absolutely no harm in Robert at all. You're misconstruing all his actions. He's always very correct, a proper, decent young doctor who takes the greatest interest in every one of us. I don't know what I would have done if he hadn't come in answer to my call last night and talked me into a calmer state of mind. I was hysterical when he arrived. You don't know what that scene with Muriel did to me. You don't seem to want to know. All you can think about is Robert!'

Cam narrowed his eyes. 'There are a lot of things I do want to know, my dear.'

Another insinuation. I felt beside myself. Then with anger I shouted, 'It isn't the first time that you've suggested that Robert and I – ' I stopped, choking.

'Yes? Robert and you?' Cam drawled.

Now I lost my control and unable to stop myself, ran to him and slapped him across the face. 'I've had enough. Take it all back. I won't have you insulting me this way. It's bad enough for you to say such awful things about an innocent doctor, but to insult *me* – suggest I deliberately coaxed Robert to come up to Quarry House in the night while you were away – oh, Cam, Cam, this can't be *you*. We *can't* be saying these things to each other.'

Without warning, I burst into tears. The next moment Cam was holding me, kissing me, begging my forgiveness. 'Darling, darling, I'm so sorry. I didn't mean it, Kate. Forgive me, darling. Say you forgive me.'

I continued sobbing because I did not know what to say or do and it was comforting being held in Cam's arms.

'Kate, I'll never forgive myself for upsetting you like this. Don't cry. I simply cannot bear to think I've made you cry.'

His distress seemed out of all proportion to the offence. He had shown his irrational jealousy of Robert, but I had actually hit him. He would not let me apologise but continued wildly accusing himself of being unworthy of me. I was learning very fast that Cam's temperament was far from being calm, placid, level, as I had supposed.

He pulled me down on the bed and lay there, stroking my hair, whispering a mixture of apologies and endearments. When he had calmed down a little I said gently, 'Darling, promise me you won't ever talk about Robert that way again. He has been very kind to me, and he wants to help us with Muriel. Whether we let him or not is not the point. What I want to establish is that you have absolutely *no reason* to mistrust his motives or mine. Robert is a doctor and a friend and that is all. You demean yourself and me by being jealous of him.'

Cam seemed to find some difficulty in controlling himself. Our bodies were so close I could feel the stiffness of his. But he spoke quietly enough. 'Very well, Kate. But you must make allowances for my feelings. He's young, attractive and...'

'Cam, *I love you!*' I interrupted him. 'Real love doesn't allow for a third person no matter how young and attractive. You haven't and never will have cause to be jealous of Robert. Won't you accept my word for it? Why can't you trust me?'

I think he was trying to do so, but I could see in his face the struggle he was having. I was shocked to realise that here was a very, very jealous man. I remembered Robert's Cathy and how, eventually, she had destroyed the relationship she had valued so much. I was afraid. Could Cam destroy us? Was I strong enough to combat this weakness in him?

'I'm your wife, Cam!' I said softly. 'You belittle the very quality of my love for you if you think it could waiver at the first hint of temptation.'

'So you admit there is a temptation?'

I felt cold. Cam was no nearer conceding the point that he had no cause to doubt me. But maybe I could turn it to my own use. 'In a way, yes!' I agreed with a calmness I certainly did not feel. 'Robert is young and attractive and nice, too. I don't deny it. I've no need to deny it, Cam. I'm in love with you. I married you and I want no one but you. Therefore the temptation Robert might present in other circumstances is quite invalid in these. Can't you see that?'

'But if you stopped loving me?'

'Cam, I don't think I *could* stop loving you, even if we both wanted it that way. It may sound crazy, but I don't think I would stop loving you even if I discovered you had killed your first two wives. Does that convince you?'

I felt him relax a little beside me. 'You mean such a hell of a lot to me, Kate. Life...well, it hasn't been too easy one way and another and I've never really known happiness until I met you. I couldn't bear to lose it...to lose you now.'

'Never, as long as we both shall live!' I vowed against his lips.

It was inevitable that when we finally made love, it was with a desperate urgency that sought to prove our love rather than to express or complete it. I don't know if Cam was aware of it, but although we were physically reunited, I felt afterwards a residue of sadness and pity for something lost.

Cam, however, was quite his old happy loving self and, as the evening wore on, I began to feel close to him again and wished very much that I need not refer once more to the unhappy subject of Muriel. So I left the problem until we were preparing to go to bed later that night. Cam had made his usual round of goodnights to the little girls and came along to our room. He wanted to know why I had put them all to sleep together. I welcomed the chance to reopen the subject of Muriel.

'Because they are less frightened than when they sleep alone,' I told him as I unzipped my dress. Cam sat in the armchair, watching me. 'Muriel has filled their heads with her dreadful tales of a ghost pushing poor Jennifer into the waterfall. No wonder they all have nightmares!'

'I don't see why it's such a "dreadful notion",' Cam argued. 'After all, it does keep them away from the waterfall and the lake, and they could be death-traps to the little ones, you know.'

I paused in the act of putting on my dressing gown. My mouth dropped open. 'You can't mean you *approve* of what Muriel has told them?'

'Well, I can't think of a more effective way of safeguarding the girls,' he said, as if it were the most normal thing in the world. 'After Jennifer's death, we were all deeply concerned about the dangers. Muriel's idea struck me as a very sensible one.'

'Then you've known – for years and years – that this was going on?'

'*What* was going on?' Cam asked, yawning.

'That she was terrorising them?'

Cam seemed more exasperated than perturbed. 'Now look, darling, you've only just come to live here. I know you are fond of the girls, and already they love you. I know you have their best interests at heart. But you must be fair. Muriel is the one who has done everything for them since their mother died. She hasn't a particularly likeable personality, and I can quite see that her sort of authority with the children can clash with your ideas. But you can't expect her to allow you to usurp her place without a bit of opposition, can you?'

I tried to stay calm. 'But Cam, you've missed the point entirely. It isn't Muriel's control of the children I object to but her methods. Of course her way is bad for them – *wrong*.' It was on the tip of my tongue to quote Robert's theory that fear was responsible for Sandra's stutter, Lillian's temperatures. I bit back the mention of Robert's name just in time and put forward the idea as my own.

'You really believe in all that psychiatric nonsense?' Cam asked, sounding genuinely curious. 'I would have thought you had sufficient intelligence not to be taken in by all that quackery.'

'But, darling, psychiatry isn't "quackery",' I protested. It just didn't seem credible that this was Cam I was talking to.

I was bitterly disappointed to find his sympathies were with Muriel. He spoke quite matter-of-factly.

'Of course it is quackery. There's far too much of it around these days. Everyone is using the subconscious as an excuse to avoid responsibility for their actions. The only people I can see benefiting from it are the doctors.'

'So you are anti the medical profession?'

Cam shrugged. 'I'm not very likely to be pro them, Kate. God knows I don't wish to revive the past but I've good cause to dislike doctors, you know. When Jennifer died, that old idiot Dr Williams damn near had me on the gallows, silly old fool. He tried to make out someone had hit Jennifer on the head before she fell in the lake. Bloody ridiculous! And in a village like this, a lot of the mud he stirred up so crazily stuck with a vengeance. It has taken years to live it down. Even now, I think old Meadows half imagines I might strangle his wife in her sleep.'

He had at last succeeded effectively in silencing me. At least I could understand now why he had an aversion to doctors as a whole. But he must keep a sense of proportion, I thought. Because of one old man's foolish mistake, Cam couldn't condemn them all. As to his views on psychiatry, they belonged to another decade.

We were strangers, I thought unhappily. Neither of us really knew much about the other. And Cam was my husband. Marriage meant the communion of two bodies and two minds, I reminded myself. I *must* somehow reach out and touch Cam's mind. If I could not do so, we would never be on the same wavelength, no matter how intensely and passionately we loved one another.

I decided to drop the subject of medicine and stick to the more vital one concerning Muriel's future. As gently as I could, I reminded him that Muriel held him responsible for her mother's death and that she believed he had harmed Jennifer, too.

I need not have worried that Cam would be hurt. He laughed – a little bitterly, perhaps, but quite genuinely unable to take the matter seriously.

'It's just her imagination running away with her!' he said, standing up and stretching. 'You can't ask me to take seriously the morbid fantasies of an adolescent girl. I certainly don't intend to do so, Kate, even if you do.'

'But, Cam, Muriel isn't an adolescent. She's eighteen!' I cried. 'Don't you *care* – that she can even *think* such things?'

'Not particularly,' Cam admitted as he began to undress. 'Ever since she was a kid, she's had these fantasies. I don't altogether blame the girl. I expect she heard some of the stories that were rife after Jennifer's death and, being imaginative, she prefers the thought of violence and mystery to the rather dull truth.'

'I thought you didn't believe in psychology,' I said sharply. 'Yet you are analysing her just as a psychiatrist would.'

'I'm doing no such thing. I'm facing facts. And while we're on the subject, I might as well confess another fact – that I've never really liked Muriel although I've always done my best for her, I hope and believe. So you see, darling, I'm not all that bothered about her opinion of me – and she knows it.'

I stared at him, confused and a little shocked. 'And you don't intend to do anything about her?'

'I'm not quite sure, Kate, what it is you are expecting me to do? Speak to the girl? Tell her to stop talking rubbish? I doubt it would do much good. I could turn her out, I suppose, but it strikes me as a little unfair after all she has done for the girls and indirectly for me. I do feel I owe her at least a roof over her head for as long as she wants it.'

'Maybe she'd like to go away – perhaps to an art college? Have a flat in town?'

Cam shrugged. 'She has only to say so. She knows I wouldn't try to stop her. But I doubt that's what she does want, Kate. She has all the facilities for her painting here. Of course, if you've really taken such a dislike to her, I'll give her a generous allowance and pack her off to London. I'm not going to have you upset this way.'

I closed my eyes. Cam and I simply were not on the same wavelength at all. He had entirely misinterpreted my feelings.

'I don't dislike her,' I said with all the patience I could muster. 'I'm just worried about her state of mind – worried that she might hurt the children, worried about the things she has said about you! I think she's ill – mentally ill. I think she needs help, professional help. I think she might even try to come between us, Cam.'

Cam came over and drew me into his arms. 'Not Muriel!' he said confidently. 'She hasn't aroused any feelings of love in you. It's those other three monkeys of mine who seem to be trying to steal your love from me. I'm much more afraid of their influence on you.'

I smiled, albeit uneasily. 'They are children, darling. You can't be jealous of my love for your children or theirs for me.'

'I'm jealous of anyone or anything which makes you one iota less mine,' Cam said fiercely. 'You're mine and only mine, Kate. Do you understand that? You're *mine!*'

For the first time in my married life, I did not want Cam to make love to me. I felt detached, shut up in my mind, as if I were another person standing there looking down on the couple locked in the most intimate embrace. This was a man, Cam Rivers, trying to prove with sheer physical passion, possession of a human being who did not wish to be so possessed. Much as I loved Cam, I felt it essential to keep my integrity, my independence of thought. I saw myself struggling feebly and ineffectually to free myself from that frightening embrace.

'I love you far more than you love me,' he said when it was over and I belonged to myself again.

I shook my head in denial, but deep down inside I had to admit that Cam could possibly be right.

Chapter Ten

I had believed that when Cam came home I could off-load all my concerns on to him. Instead, I had acquired another one – Cam himself. I now knew I had to guard and protect him in much the same way as I did his three little girls. He was the most insecure of them all, and I wasn't going to help him by trying to convince him that Muriel was in some way a danger, a threat to us. He was too accustomed to her and her ways. He did not want to be involved – perhaps because it would revive memories of his unhappy past. But what could I do on my own? I could not allow the existing state of affairs to continue. It was inconceivable to me that Cam could accept them as a matter of course.

The thought of Joanne, who had always been a kind of replacement mother to me, came as a bright shaft of sunshine on a rainy day. I resolved that when I returned to London with Cam on Monday, I would go and see her.

I decided to write her a letter to prepare her for my visit. Joanne was a very social person. I did not want her to be out when I called.

I scribbled a quick note, stuck it in an envelope, and went to find Cam to tell him I was going to the post office.

He was helping the little girls in the summer-house. The smile with which he had greeted my arrival changed to a frown when I spoke. 'You're going to the village? Why? What letter?'

I held out my letter to Joanne. To my surprise, Cam took it from me and scrutinised the envelope.

'I thought I'd let Joanne know I'd be in London next week so we can make a date to meet,' I told him. He handed me back the envelope with that same suspicious expression on his face I had seen last night.

'What do you want to go to the village for? You can give it to the postman when he calls at four o'clock.'

I explained that if there were no incoming mail, the postman might not stop. I wished Joanne to get my letter by Monday. Besides, I needed some stamps.

'Why? What's the hurry?' Cam persisted. 'If you're seeing her next week, I don't see the necessity for writing at all.'

The conversation simply did not make sense to me. I could think of no reason why Cam should object to my writing to Joanne. Furthermore, I resented his interference.

'If I wish to write to her, I will!' I said, sharply.

Cam took a step toward me which I can only describe as threatening. His face betrayed an emotion I took to be anger. 'You will *not* go down to the village!' he ordered.

Desperately, I tried to think what possible reason Cam could have to keep me away from the village. Suddenly I guessed what might be wrong. The post office was adjacent to the doctor's surgery. Was it possible Cam thought I was using the letter as an excuse to go and see Robert? I fought back my own anger and sense of injustice and with great self-control, said coolly, 'Why don't you come down to the village with me, darling? It's a lovely day and you'd enjoy the walk.'

For a moment, suspicion lingered in his eyes. Then he smiled, a warm, loving smile. 'You're quite right, I would like a walk.'

Perhaps it was as well the children came too, for I would have found it hard to make casual conversation with Cam. As it was, the girls took most of his attention, and I was free to fight my feelings. I had been frightened by the intensity of Cam's anger; frightened, too, by that threatening look on his face when I defied him. This violence in him was new to me, and I didn't know how to cope with it.

For the second time in as many hours, I began to wonder if I were having delusions. To see Cam at this moment, gentle, loving, smiling at one child or the other, laughing, joking, teasing, it was impossible to believe in that other man, consumed with a jealousy so intense that he had actually wanted to strike me. It was no good pretending otherwise. He had been angry enough to want to hit me. What would happen, I wondered, if ever I gave Cam real cause for jealousy? The thought was frightening enough in itself.

Walking beside Cam and his children, I asked myself now, if I would still have married him had I known of this twisted side to his nature before I became committed. I decided that I would have. I loved him. There was also a strong maternal streak in my nature that was struggling to the surface. I wanted to help him in exactly the same way as I would have wanted to help him overcome a more obvious physical handicap. Somehow I must combat this terrible feeling of estrangement. I must get to know and accept this new Cam and stop feeling shocked, hurt, alone, every time he behaved so badly. If I could not do this – step across the barrier to meet him, stay close to him – then we would grow further and further apart.

It was easy enough to theorise in this way, but even with the resolve fresh in my mind, I was not up to putting my ideas into practice. As we entered the village a car drew up beside us and I heard, of all people, Robert's voice calling a cheerful greeting.

'I didn't expect to see you!' he said, leaning out of the open car window. 'Nice surprise! How's Mrs Meadows? How are you, Mr Rivers? Beautiful day!'

My natural instinct was to return Robert's friendly smile, to answer his greetings, but I stood still, silent, waiting for Cam to make at least a polite reply. But he ignored Robert, moving off down the Street as though neither Robert, the car, nor I existed.

So many different emotions shot through me then that I remained paralysed, my mouth stupidly hanging open in shocked surprise. That Cam could have been so rude as deliberately to cut our doctor who had stopped to call a friendly good-day was beyond me.

At last I found my voice. 'I'm sorry, Robert!' I apologised and set off half-running to catch up with Cam and the children. Cam's face looked thunderous. I saw a look of bewilderment on little Lillian's face as she said, obviously not for the first time, 'But, Daddy, it was *Dr Carnes!* Why can't we stay and talk to him? I like him.'

Cam growled back at her, 'Will you please shut up! This minute, Lillian!'

I was conscious of Robert's car passing us. From the corner of my eye, I noted that he did not now turn his head. Well, I told myself bitterly, one could hardly wonder that he was offended. I was so angry with Cam that if the children had not been with us, I would have lost my temper.

We reached the post office. In silence I posted my letter to Joanne, more than glad I had written to her. I had never been more in need of sound common sense and advice. The children sensed the tautness of the atmosphere and were silent. Even when Cam, in a perfectly normal voice, told them they could buy sweets, they remained quiet and subdued.

On the walk back, I deliberately dropped behind Cam and I felt Lillian's hot, sticky hand feel its way into mine. This pathetic little gesture demanding comfort and security renewed my anger with Cam, the more so since I knew I too was behaving badly. Not even for the children's sake could I bring myself to walk beside Cam and carry on a normal conversation.

When we reached Quarry House, I went straight up to our room. Cam followed me a moment later. He did not try to touch me, but crossed to the window and stood staring down into the garden. 'I suppose you hate me now!' he muttered.

This childish statement threw my emotions once more into chaos. My anger subsided and a kind of helpless incomprehension caught hold of me, leaving me speechless. This man, my husband, so much older than I, had spoken as Lillian might have done when she knew she had committed some offence: *'I suppose you hate me now!'*.

'You must admit it did look suspicious,' Cam went on, more as if he were talking to himself than to me. 'You wanting to go to the village to post that damn letter and then Carnes riding past just as if he'd been expecting you. You must admit, Kate, it *looked* suspicious!'

'Cam, I love you!'

Now he was aware again of my existence. He turned and came quickly towards me, his face drawn with unhappiness. He sat down on the bed beside me and said, 'I'm sorry, darling, *I'm sorry*. I'll make it up to you. I'll ring him up and apologise if you like. I'll ask him up for drinks. I'll do anything you say!'

'Oh, Cam!' I felt tears stinging the back of my eyes. 'Can't you see, I don't *care* about Robert. I only care that you should suffer this way. You've got to trust me. You've got to trust my love for you. If we go on like this...'

'I know, I know. I'm sorry, darling!'

I held him in my arms and tried desperately not to feel frightened. I had married a man I thought would take care of me, whom I could respect, lean on, love. Now I was discovering I had married a child, and I wasn't at all sure I could cope.

Somehow, we managed to reach a normal plane again by the time we joined the children for nursery tea. Cam seemed able to recover quickly from these bouts and I tried hard to do the same. It was as if he had a child's capacity to jump from one mood to another. But he had not forgotten the incident. Before dinner he insisted that I telephone Robert. I did not want to do so.

'But you must, Kate. Tell Carnes I didn't recognise him. You can make it all right. Go on, darling, please. I won't feel it's right between you and me until you do.'

'But, Cam...'

I broke off. Maybe it would be better to let him believe the problem could be solved so easily. I was sure it could not.

Robert's voice, when I got through to him, was reassuringly normal. Conscious of Cam standing near at hand, I began my apology but Robert cut me short.

'Of course, Kate. Think no more of it. I quite understand. Anything in particular you wanted to chat about? Muriel? Does your husband want me to see her?'

Cam's presence tied my tongue.

'I don't think so,' I said guardedly. 'Cam feels I've been making too much of Muriel's...nonsense!' The word came out with difficulty. 'He says she has always been imaginative and tends to exaggerate everything. I'm sorry I called you out unnecessarily the other night.'

Robert must have guessed Cam was near at hand. He knew me well enough by now to realise that I couldn't be expressing my own views. He said: 'It wasn't unnecessarily, Kate. Let me know if I can be of help – any time. Okay?'

'Fine! And thanks!'

I put the receiver down with relief. Cam's face was relaxed, smiling.

'There, I told you it would be all right. Now we can forget him and Muriel and be happy, eh?'

I could neither forget – how could I – or be happy. So long as I could not speak openly and honestly to Cam, we would live in separate worlds. But this was not the moment to try to establish an understanding. I resolved to wait until we were alone in London. There, without interruptions or distractions from the children, Cam might be able to see things more realistically. I had two problems really: his growing jealousy and Muriel.

My longing to confide in Joanne increased with every hour that brought me nearer to London and normality. Even my distress at saying good-bye to the three little girls was swamped by my need to see Joanne; to be able to share the load on my mind. Lillian's tears and Debbie's hugs were pushed to the back of my thoughts, together with Sandra's stuttered 'W-w-when w-will you c-c-come b-b-back, Kate? You w-w-will c-c-come b-b-back, w-w-won't you?'

Yet far away from them all and when finally I was curled up in my old bucket-shaped armchair in the familiar sitting room that had once been my home, I was silent. Shoes off, a tea tray between us, Joanne's interested, sympathetic face gazing at me expectantly, I yet said nothing.

'Well, come on, luv!' she prompted. 'Let's hear all about it. Your letter sounded as if you were positively dying to off-load.'

So I told her about Quarry House, about the summer-house, about the garden, the countryside, Mrs Meadows, even Robert. I talked and talked – yet never of Cam, never of Muriel.

When finally I stopped Joanne gave me an odd sideways glance and said, 'Your life down there sounds like something out of a gothic novel. You are happy, aren't you, luv? There's nothing wrong? You mentioned a few problems in your letter. Serious ones, I think you said.'

'But of course I'm happy. Cam adores me and I have everything in the world I need.'

Even to my own ears, I did not sound convincing. I tried once more to tell Joanne what the problems were. But the words would not come. Here, in the very normality of my surroundings, the place I had longed for and rediscovered with delight and relief, I felt that what I had to say would sound so fantastic, even I would doubt the implications. I could almost laugh at them myself. Murders, ghosts, screaming children, demented girls, my fear, Cam's jealousy – Joanne would think me insane if I spoke of such things, and have good justification for it.

I prevaricated. 'I do sometimes worry a bit about Cam,' I said. Deliberately I chose a vague, unconcerned tone of voice. 'He gets a bit aroused – you know, Joanne – annoyed if I pay too much attention to anyone else.'

'Your doctor, for example?'

I attempted a smile. 'For one – yes!' I agreed.

'Well, can you blame Cam?' Joanne said, always reasonable. 'Your letter described the local medico as "dishy". Hardly a view a newlywed husband might appreciate from his pretty young bride!'

'But, Joanne, I *love* Cam and he knows I do. Robert is nothing more than a friend. You can't really be so old-fashioned as to suggest a married woman should have no men friends?'

'Not I!' said Joanne. 'But I wouldn't blame Cam for feeling a bit jealous. I know there's no cause for it but let's face it, you are very attractive, Kate – more so than you seem to realise. Marriage has almost made you beautiful. If I were Cam, I think I'd resent you even blinking an eyelash at your young doctor.'

I let it go. Not even to Joanne could I betray the childish and unreasonable scenes I had with Cam about Robert. I didn't want her to think badly of him and my loyalty to him superseded my need to confide in her for my own peace of mind. Besides, I wanted to believe her view that Cam's behaviour was normal.

Joanne pumped me a bit more about Robert. She said he sounded nice, that she'd come down and stay with us soon if Cam and I would invite her, and see if she couldn't bring a little fun and excitement into Robert's life. I knew they'd like each other, become good friends, but that was all. I tried to think of Robert and Joanne in a matchmaking way, but couldn't. I warmed to the idea of Joanne coming down. It would be marvellous to have her at Quarry House. Yet, at the same time, I wasn't sure I would invite her even if Cam were willing. Joanne was very astute. She would almost certainly see deeper than the superficials. I disliked this new feeling that I had something to hide.

I am sure Joanne guessed there was a great deal more on my mind than I revealed at the time. But I believe I succeeded in steering her away from my problems as I sat there giving her word portraits of the children, explaining how and why I had come to love them.

Joanne grinned. 'Can't say I ever thought of you as particularly maternal,' she teased me, 'but I suppose now it's only a matter of time before you start producing a second batch of chicks for Cam.'

'He'd like a son!' I agreed. But a cold shiver touched my skin to goose pimples. Cam might say he wanted me to have his son and heir, believing it in theory. But what about in practice? Would he resent a baby when it challenged him for my time and attention? My love?

'I don't want a baby for ages yet,' I told Joanne hurriedly. 'I need to get accustomed to being a wife first. Even now it isn't all that easy for Cam and me to be alone together at Quarry House.'

Joanne seemed to accept this without question.

'Well, it's good for you to be away from the brood for a bit,' she said. 'You look pale, luv. You need a rest.'

I nearly weakened again then; nearly told Joanne that it wasn't so much a physical rest I needed as a quiet mind. And this eluded me the whole of the five days I was in London alone with Cam. I wanted to forget Quarry House and the children, to revive the carefree honeymoon atmosphere; but I discovered that no matter how far I had travelled in distance, my problems went with me. No matter how successfully I pushed my worries to the very back of my mind, they were still there, dark, sinister, and insoluble.

Chapter Eleven

Time succeeded where distance could not. Soon after our week in London, the school vacation came to an end and I was caught up in the mundane but exacting task of marking and mending items of the girls' uniforms and packing their school trunks.

Mrs Meadows was fully operative again when finally Cam and I drove the little girls up to London to catch the school train, leaving Muriel and Quarry House behind us for the next three months. We planned to spend an occasional weekend up there, weather permitting, but to base ourselves in the town flat until the little ones were home from school again for Christmas.

I felt only a pang of guilt at leaving Muriel by herself in that huge house. When I asked her if she would be lonely, she merely gave me that curious half-smile of hers and said that on the contrary she would welcome the peace. There was always Logan if she needed a companion.

I failed completely to understand Muriel's relationship with Logan Winter. Rather like some pale ghost, I would catch glimpses of him crossing the courtyard or gliding down one of the passages of Quarry House. Muriel seldom invited him to a family meal, no doubt aware that Cam did not find anything in common with him. If she resented our unspoken antipathy to Logan, she did not show it, but

I believed she saw him frequently in her studio. It surprised me that I never noticed him actually going into the stable or leaving it, yet occasionally heard his voice, high-pitched and somewhat effeminate, talking to Muriel in the studio. If anything, I believed they were more like brother and sister than lovers, and having no other close friends, depended upon each other in their isolation for companionship.

Selfishly, no doubt, I soon forgot both Logan and Muriel. Despite the fact that I was now stepmother to four girls, I, too, was young and was soon caught up again in London life. I saw a lot of Joanne and looked up many of my other friends. I shopped and treated myself to a new hairdo, a facial, and a lot of new clothes. I discovered for the first time the pleasures of being married to a man who could afford to give me as much as I could possibly want in the way of a personal allowance. Cam seemed delighted when I showed any propensity towards extravagance.

No woman could have had a more appreciative or attentive husband. He never failed to remark upon a new dress or hairstyle and was always giving me presents – jewellery, flowers, a little gold watch for evenings, a beautiful leather coat, and a fun fur for every day. He was quite fantastically generous and, like any girl, I thrilled to this new orgy of spending. I went to shops I could never afford to go to before. I bought some lovely clothes for the children. I bought ties and sweaters and pyjamas for Cam and together we chose some new pieces of furniture for Quarry House. Cam said I could have a completely free hand to do as I pleased in the house, and I did particularly want to modernise the big kitchen. So I used up a great deal of time wandering from store to store looking at units and planning how I would arrange them.

In the evenings Cam took me to theatres, concerts, the ballet or cinema, and sometimes just to dine and dance.

Only occasionally did he show signs of the old jealousy. If I were not in the flat when he arrived home from work, he questioned me minutely as to my activities as if he feared I'd been on some illicit assignation. But this, too, lessened as time wore on and my accounting of my shopping sprees soon reassured Cam that I was not renewing friendships with erstwhile boyfriends.

There was only one quite absurd but serious upset: it arose one evening when the hall porter, Judd, with whom I had established a firm friendship, paid me a compliment as I was leaving with Cam to go to the theatre.

'Have a good time, duck,' he said as I wished him goodnight. 'You really do look a treat, if I may say so.'

Old Judd must have been nearing seventy. He was completely bald with a red, shining pate and face. He had a great-grandchild. I used to tease him, telling him he looked far too young and attractive to be a great-grandfather. I simply could not believe it when, in the taxi leaving the building, Cam gave me a thunderous glance and said, 'Bloody cheek, talking to you like that. I'll get that man fired. About time he learned his place.'

I rose in old Judd's defence without thought for my words. The very last thing Judd lacked was respect. I told Cam so.

'I won't have anyone speaking to you in that familiar way!' Cam stormed. 'Who does he think he is? I can see the way he looks at you. I won't have it. I'll see he gets sacked.'

Only then did I realise that this was the ugly side of Cam's nature emerging once more. It didn't seem believable that he could be jealous of the poor old man. Cam's insinuations were so ridiculous that I should have been able to laugh at them. Judd often told me I reminded him of one of his granddaughters now living in Australia. He treated me exactly as a kindly old grandfather might do, telling me not to get my feet wet or to have a nice cup of tea if he thought I looked tired.

Quietly, reasonably, I tried to explain this to Cam. But he would not retract. He ceased arguing the point but remained for the rest of the evening in a dark, sullen mood with which finally I lost patience.

When we reached home, I shut Cam out of our bedroom, and pointedly put his pillow and pyjamas on the big settee in the drawing-room. I suppose it was a silly thing to do, but I was tired and very upset and it seemed a reasonable gesture at the time. But when he found the door locked against him, he went completely wild, shouting and kicking at it and telling me that if I did not let him in, he'd 'break the damn thing down'.

Frightened by the violence of his reaction, I finally turned the key. Cam's face was white with fury as he came towards me with that same horrifying look in his eyes I'd seen once before – as if he hated me. His hands were clenched into fists and it crossed my mind that he was about to hit me.

Instinct warned me not to oppose him by word or deed. He was almost out of control. I remained motionless and silent.

Then, like a collapsed balloon, he went limp. The anger left him. He pulled me into his arms and held me so tightly against him I had to fight for breath. I heard his voice against my hair. 'Forgive me, forgive me. I love you, Kate. You don't begin to know how much I love you. Forgive me, darling. I didn't mean to frighten you. I'd die if you ever left me. I couldn't bear it. I love you, I love you. I'd kill you first. I'd kill myself. Oh, Kate, help me. Forgive me. Love me!'

But although I went through the motions of love, spoke words of love, performed the actions of love, I was emotionally numbed with shock. I could not reconcile that crazy, uncontrolled man with the distinguished, self-assured, intelligent Cam whom I had fallen in love with and married. His day-to-day nature was always gentle, full of care for me. I thought of the door locked against him and promised myself never to do this again. This strange dark side to his nature seemed to spring from fear that I might stop loving him. I must never again give him cause to think this could happen.

The following morning Cam seemed absolutely normal. I was not able to find my own equilibrium so quickly. I had a splitting headache and after Cam had gone, I went back to bed. But I could not relax. I felt too far out of my depth. I longed suddenly for Robert and his good counsel. I felt I must have help. Robert was the obvious person to confide in. He knew Cam, me, the family. Perhaps he would tell me the best way to behave to help Cam.

I jumped out of bed and found paper and pen. At first the words would not come. It felt as if I were being disloyal to Cam, telling a third person of his weaknesses. But I reminded myself Robert was a doctor – Cam's doctor as well as mine. Then the sentences poured from me. I referred back to the letter-posting incident when I had last seen Robert and Cam's behaviour had been so disproportionate. I referred to his strange attitude to Muriel and his reluctance to take her seriously. I ended by asking Robert to advise me what I should do now, if anything.

As I read the letter and placed it in an envelope, I realised I dared not give the flat as an address to which Robert could reply. Cam would see the Yorkshire postmark and instantly demand to know whom my letter was from. He was always inquisitive about my mail; phone calls, too.

Resentment replaced my anxiety. Cam had no right to constitute himself my jailer, for that was how it seemed to me now. It was humiliating for me to know he had so little faith in me. Now, for the first time, I decided to live up – or was it down? – to his low opinion of me; I would go behind his back, not because I wished to be deceitful, but because he himself had made it impossible for me to be honest.

I took the letter out of the envelope and furiously scribbled a postscript asking Robert to write to me care of Joanne and giving her address. Then I dressed and hurried downstairs, pushed the letter into Judd's hand, and asked him to post it for me at once. I hurried because I was afraid I might have second thoughts. Once the letter was gone I couldn't retrieve it.

Joanne teased me a bit on the phone when finally she rang to say there was a 'mysterious missive' awaiting my collection.

'I presume you don't want it forwarded?' she added.

I felt miserably disloyal to Cam as I told Joanne I'd call to collect the letter from her.

Robert's reply was cautiously and carefully worded. I should not have expected anything else. He couldn't know for sure whether his letter might not fall into Cam's hands. He said he could not diagnose from such indirect evidence and did not feel justified in giving any opinion or advice other than to caution me very seriously about offering Cam further provocation.

I have first-hand experience of the subject you raised, as you know. Any uncontrolled emotion is potentially dangerous, this in particular. I do feel you should make every attempt to seek professional advice. I am convinced that it is needed even while I see that this might not be easy for you to achieve.

Try to keep calm yourself. This is the best and safest way to help. And be on your guard, Kate. Avoid direct confrontations before they can develop. When do you return here? I could be of greater help if we could talk about this.

I took the liberty (wonderful phrase!) of calling at Quarry House ostensibly to see how Mrs Meadows was getting on but really to check on Muriel for you. I'm glad to say she seemed quite herself, busy painting, I gathered, and seeing a fair bit of the Winter boy. I am forced to agree with you that he's not a very attractive personality!

Do you have a London doctor? If so, perhaps you could call him in on some pretext concerning yourself and ask his help since I am virtually unable to help from here. I would feel a lot easier in my mind if you could do this.

Keep in touch.

Ever your friend,

ROBERT.

His reply left me far from comforted. I suppose I had hoped he would tell me, as Joanne had, not to worry; that Cam's was the perfectly normal, if slightly exaggerated, behaviour of a possessive man very much in love. I don't know what I really expected to hear, but I had not anticipated the cold shiver of fear that followed Robert's cautious warning. His obvious concern for my safety merely increased my own feelings of unease.

Joanne, watching my face as I read my letter, must have seen my dismay. She asked anxiously, 'Everything okay, luv?'

I nodded. Loyalty to Cam would not let me confide in her though I longed to do so.

Joanne, bless her, did not pursue the subject.

'The letter is from Robert,' I volunteered. 'He thought I'd like to know he'd been up at Quarry House to see Muriel and that all was well.'

Joanne raised her eyebrows.

'Any reason why all shouldn't be well?' she queried.

At long last I felt free to talk openly; to explain my antipathy to Cam's stepdaughter and describe her odd behaviour and beliefs. I glossed over Muriel's ridiculous idea that Cam was in some way responsible for her mother's and Jennifer's deaths.

Joanne listened quietly, reading between the lines, I think. But she kept her opinions to herself and seemed to accept my summing up that Muriel was unbalanced but that Cam was too accustomed to her odd behaviour to notice it as I did.

The only comment Joanne made was that since Muriel was not Cam's child, I was under no obligation to try to like or understand her.

'Now Cam has you to care for the little girls, Muriel will probably leave home to make her own life,' she suggested.

I doubted it. Muriel seemed quite happy where she was, but I didn't argue the point with Joanne. I didn't really expect her to appreciate my feelings about Muriel, never having met her. Besides, I really didn't have time to bother about Muriel. I was too concerned about Cam.

I worried for a few days and then, as December approached, my anxiety was pushed to the back of my mind while I grappled with Christmas shopping. I discovered the immense pleasure of buying for children. Everywhere I went, I haunted toy departments and bought so many things for the little ones that Cam laughingly told me they'd need mattress covers instead of stockings.

It was more difficult choosing for Muriel. I knew the children's tastes, but I found I did not know Muriel's at all. I settled finally for a locket containing an antique hand-painted miniature. I felt this could not fail to please any artist. It was expensive but beautiful.

We made only one weekend visit to Quarry House before the holidays. I had looked forward to it but, once there, the house seemed too large and empty without the children, despite Mrs Meadows' efforts to make it look cheerful. There were huge fires in the drawing-room and dining-room. The floors and furniture shone with her polishing efforts, and old Meadows had done his best to provide flowering plants. The house was really beautiful – but empty. Even the little dogs seemed quiet and subdued once they had given us their riotous welcome.

Autumn mists hung over the gardens and the lake. The trees were bare and gaunt and the hills hidden in low clouds. No wonder the villagers believed the house was haunted, I thought. Even I could believe in ghosts, seeing the house so desolate.

Cam kept busy dealing with household and business affairs. With time on my hands, I looked for Muriel. I had never before been to her studio uninvited, but now I crossed over the yard to the stables and knocked on her door.

She was not painting but writing. She sat on the divan, pen poised, sheets of paper strewn around her. When she saw me she nodded in a not unfriendly way and told me to find myself a chair.

The studio was cold. I must have shivered because Muriel said, 'Sorry I can't offer you more heat. It would spoil the paint, you see. Keep your coat on; I should.'

'I thought you might be painting,' I said, huddling in the stained armchair, as near as I could get to the small black stove which offered only a glimmer of warmth.

'Light's too bad.' Muriel said laconically. 'When it's like this, I write.'

'I didn't know you wrote as well as painted,' I said. 'May I ask about the literary masterpiece?'

Muriel gave me that half smile of hers.

'By all means! It's a history of Quarry House during the occupation of the Rivers family. One day people will want to know – *everything*. It's all down here in black and white.'

I don't know why her words frightened me but they did. Her voice was quiet and level yet there was a veiled threat behind it. In cowardly fashion I turned the conversation aside.

'Did you ever finish my portrait?' I asked.

Muriel nodded and stretching like a beautiful lazy cat, uncrossed her legs and stood up.

'I'll show you!'

She walked across the room and drew back a shabby curtain covering part of the wall. It was so dark that I could see little from where I sat other than that three pictures hung there.

'There you are – Mrs Rivers the Third!' Muriel said with a low laugh. 'Want to see? Come closer.'

I didn't want to see. I wanted to run out of the studio and never go near the place again. But there was a challenge in Muriel's voice which made me stay. Forcing myself to be calm, I got up and strolled over to join Muriel.

There I was in oils, looking childish, insipid, almost vacuous. I looked out upon the world as a halfwit might stare at something it did not understand. Pretty, yes! Intelligent, no! Cleverly, Muriel had obtained a good likeness and yet made me look an idiot. But why?

I wanted to turn away, but I would not let myself. I said casually, 'I don't think it's a good likeness, Muriel!' I turned to the other portraits. Jennifer – looking just as she looked in that photograph in the children's room – plump, plain, matronly, kind, but again, stupid. There was that same fatuous devoted expression in her eyes as in mine. But for the difference in shape and colour, our eyes could have been interchanged.

With curiosity I turned to the portrait of Muriel's mother. Here there was a total opposite. In the lean, angular beautiful face lay a keen intelligence. The mouth was bitter and hard. It was the portrait of a woman who had seen all that was worst in life and had no illusions left.

It was a tragic, bitter face. It was also extraordinarily like Muriel's.

Now I did close my eyes – to hide what I could barely bring myself to look upon. I heard Muriel beside me, saying triumphantly, 'So you do see the difference, Kate! At least you have artistic perception!' She laughed. 'I can see it upsets you – frightens you a little, too, doesn't it? Well, now you've seen them all – The Three Victims, I call them.'

I went back to my chair, struggling harder than ever now not to turn and run. Marshalling all my self-control, I said, 'That's such a ridiculous way to talk, Muriel. I know you believe your stepfather was responsible for your mother's death. You were just a child at the time, and such thoughts are excusable only on that score. But you are grown-up now and, I think, intelligent. You cannot go on believing such ridiculous nonsense. Your stepfather doesn't take it seriously, and I think he's quite right. It's ludicrous. Moreover, I don't care to hear you talk about him that way or to know that you can even think on those lines. You must see how absurd it is.'

Muriel did not seem in the least perturbed by my outspokenness. She merely shrugged her shoulders and said, 'It isn't I who am deluded, Kate. You are so much in love you cannot see the plain facts for yourself. I know. You are merely guessing.'

She let the curtain fall back over the pictures and resumed her place on the divan.

'On the contrary, Muriel, I am the one facing the facts and you are the one living in a dream world – or perhaps I should call it a nightmare world. The facts are painful but simple – your mother met with an awful and tragic accident, and so did Jennifer. There were inquests on both of these deaths, and the verdict in each case exonerated Cam completely. Anything sinister lies only in your imagination.'

'You really believe those verdicts, don't you? That's because you don't want to believe anything else. But I know the truth, Kate. I can show you proof, but you wouldn't want to see it. You don't want to know any more than Jennifer did. You are in love, and you couldn't go on loving a man you knew was a murderer, could you?'

'You're sick!' I said. 'So much so that I'm very deeply concerned about you. I want to help you. Would you let me, Muriel? Would you come to see a doctor if I could arrange it? Someone who could straighten everything out for you?'

'This conversation is rather a waste of time, isn't it?' Muriel replied. 'Logan warned me it would be useless and he's right. You don't want to know the truth. But I thought I just *might* persuade you to look at my mother's diary. I was wrong.'

'Muriel, if such a diary existed and did mention something that incriminated your stepfather, why didn't you produce it when Jennifer died? That's what you want, isn't it? To make Cam pay for your mother's death? You really believe he was responsible and you intend somehow to make him pay for it?'

'I don't believe. I *know!*' Muriel said in that same flat voice.

I cannot think how I continued such a conversation. At the time it shocked me but it did not seem so outrageous as it does now when I look back on it. The thought of Cam driving one woman to suicide and murdering another was so stupid and ridiculous that I was now convinced of Muriel's insanity.

'Let me see the diary!' I said quietly. 'I'm not in the least afraid to see it, Muriel. In fact, I very much doubt that it even exists.'

Muriel's face looked guarded. 'It exists all right. But can I trust you not to give it to Father?'

'Don't be silly! It's your property and, if you lent it to me, I would return it to you without showing it to anyone. Though why Cam should *not* see it I don't fully understand.'

'Don't you? He might destroy it, and it's a vital part of the proof.'

Now I began to feel genuinely sorry for the girl. She really did believe what she was saying and I could no longer be angry, even for Cam's sake, with someone so deranged.

'Let me see the diary,' I said gently. 'I give you my word I will return it. If it would make you any happier, I'll read it here and now in the studio.'

I thought I had called her bluff, that there would be no diary. I felt the first twinge of uneasiness when Muriel got up promptly and went to the desk near the window. She unlocked the centre drawer and took out a small leather-bound book.

'There it is – take it! Now perhaps there's at least a chance of saving your life!'

And she thrust the book into my trembling hands.

Chapter Twelve

'So you have actually persuaded her to read it!' Logan Winter's voice, coming from behind my shoulder, startled me so completely I had to bite back a scream.

I swung round to face him and said furiously, 'How long have you been eavesdropping?'

Logan's pale face twisted in what might have been a smile but looked more like a sneer. 'Muriel and I don't have any secrets so I'd scarcely need to eavesdrop, would I?'

Muriel, I noticed, looked angry. But she said nothing.

'I didn't hear you come in, Logan.' I sounded accusing, but I didn't care.

My words produced an unexpected silence. Muriel and Logan were exchanging glances I could not interpret. Then Muriel said placatingly, 'I'm sorry you were startled, Kate. I'm sure Logan didn't mean to scare you. Are you all right? You look terribly pale.'

I was not sure if she were laughing at me or genuinely solicitous. But that was not unusual. I never did know what the girl meant or felt.

Suddenly an odd thought shot across my mind. I had been standing by the window while I'd been talking to Muriel, staring down into the courtyard as I listened to her. Yet I had not seen Logan approaching the stables.

Muriel guessed my thoughts with uncanny perception. She said quickly, 'Logan came by the secret passage. Hasn't Father told you about it? I should have thought he would – or maybe he didn't want you to know of its existence.'

More ambiguities. Unwittingly, my legs gave way and I sat down heavily on the paint-streaked divan.

'Perhaps you'd be good enough to explain,' I said with difficulty. My tongue seemed too big for my mouth.

Once again, Muriel exchanged glances with Logan. Then he walked away to the far end of the studio, and Muriel sat down beside me.

'The passage runs from the wine cellar under the kitchen to a trapdoor beneath the harness room. Years ago, the priests used it during the days of religious persecution. Most old houses had hideaways or passages such as this one at Quarry House. A lot were bricked up, and no one knows of their existence. Father discovered ours when he was having the house renovated soon after his marriage to my mother.'

While she spoke, my fear had given way to interest; now curiosity was supplanted by trepidation. Why hadn't Cam told me about the passage? He had been so enthusiastic when he'd first shown me over the house, pointing out everything of historical interest. He could not have forgotten such a fascinating part of it!

Again Muriel read my thoughts accurately. She said, 'I simply don't understand why Father omitted to show you the passage. Naturally, I assumed he had or I'd have shown you myself.'

I remained silent, unable to think of a valid explanation. From the far end of the room, Logan spoke. 'Perhaps he didn't want Kate to know about the escape route.'

His insinuation was too obvious to be overlooked. He, like Muriel, believed Cam intended to harm me. But I had no intention of arguing the point with Logan Winter. I ignored his remark and said to Muriel, 'Do show me the way, Muriel. I'd love to see a secret passage. It sounds like something out of a fairy tale.'

I sounded stupid, but I did not care. I wanted to get out of the studio, and I wanted to see if this passage was a reality.

Muriel looked bored but nevertheless said she would lead the way. 'You may need to use it, Kate, so I'd better show you, I suppose.'

I succeeded in withholding my anger, reminding myself that this girl was sick and not to be taken literally.

Logan did not get up as I followed Muriel down the staircase to the harness room. I was glad. I found his company even less congenial than Muriel's. She opened a trapdoor of thick wood with two heavy rings and hinges set deep in it. A rush of cold musty air came up from the darkness below. Muriel bent down and took a large torch from a shelf just inside the opening.

'I'll lead the way!' she said briefly, and switching on the torch, shone the light deep into the darkness of the tunnel.

It was roughly hewn from the limestone that I knew lay just below the ground on which Quarry House had been built. In years gone by there had been several large quarries here, one of which had been flooded to make the lake. The other two had been filled in when the quarries closed down.

Water seeped through cracks in the stone walls and roof, and a damp mould covered everything. It was chill and dank.

I followed a few steps behind Muriel, trying not to give way to fear. If she were to turn suddenly and strike me with that heavy torch, I had nothing with which to defend myself. I could turn and run, but Logan Winter would be waiting for me at the passage entrance, and I had little doubt that he and Muriel were, for good or evil, mutually committed.

We seemed to walk for miles but, in fact, it was only a few minutes before the passage began to slope upward and became stone steps. Finally we emerged in the wine cellar beneath the kitchen of Quarry House.

Mrs Meadows, like some welcome familiar angel of warmth and normality, was baking scones. She greeted us cheerfully and told me Cam was looking for me.

But I was not yet ready to see Cam. First I wanted to read the diary.

I thanked Muriel for showing me the passage and ran up to the empty nursery. I wanted to be alone, and I knew Cam would not look for me there.

The pages of Margaret Rivers' diary were thumb-marked and dog-eared. Muriel had obviously read and reread them. Pencil lines underscored any words which bore even a likely reference to Cam's blame for the suicidal theme that ran through it.

If I could go back in time and refuse to read that book, I would. Maybe then everything would have turned out differently. I sometimes think so and yet, remembering that afternoon in Muriel's studio and the conversation which led up to my demand to see the diary, Fate intended it this way.

I could quote from memory long passages which remain in my mind, but I prefer to forget them. The whole diary was a horrible insight into the mind of a woman poisoned by her own insatiable greed.

I did not have to read far to discover Margaret Rivers' motive in marrying Cam. Money and the desire for it were an obsession. The daughter of a penniless vicar, lonely and deprived as a child of all luxuries, she had determined early on in her life to marry money. Mistakenly, she ran away with a man, Muriel's father, who had seemed at the time to represent all that she wanted but, as she was all too soon to discover, turned out to be a flashy, none too successful salesman. He did at least marry her when he learned she was pregnant, but left her penniless long before the child was born.

Margaret Rivers had been too proud to go home and beg for shelter from the parents who had turned their backs on her when she left home to live with such a man. Also, she had no desire to exchange one kind of poverty for another. She became a waitress in a men's club in London and being young, attractive and well-spoken, soon acquired a protector, a well-to-do businessman. He supplied her with a flat which permitted her to reclaim her baby from the foster home where she had placed it in order to go to work. When the child was two years old, she met Cam. The moment she discovered he had money, she made up her mind she would marry him.

The innocence of the old vicarage days had long since disappeared. She had learned at lot about men from her protector. She set about her campaign to win Cam with shrewdness and success. Only twenty-two at the time and still raw after an unhappy affair with a girl at Cambridge, Cam soon became infatuated with Margaret, now a sophisticated, attractive woman some years his senior.

She took a calculated risk and lied to Cam, pretending that her protector was deeply in love with her and wanted to marry her. It was not such a gamble, taking into account the fact that she had discovered Cam was very possessive and jealous. At once he proposed marriage, promising to take her and the child away from all the sordid unhappiness of their present life to the safety and beauty of his estate in Yorkshire.

There was little doubt in my mind as I reached this stage of the diary that all Margaret demanded from her marriage was money; all Cam really wanted was total possession of

Margaret's body. Her attraction for him was undoubtedly physical. They had nothing otherwise in common. Inevitably once the novelty of marriage wore off, Cam's passion began to wane. There were rows over money. Margaret demanded that he make over a large sum of money to her and he refused. Each row alienated them further and now, suddenly, the emphasis changed. While Margaret had held the reins when Cam was so urgently and passionately demanding, now that he no longer desired her, she wanted him. She fell in love with him. The emotion consumed her as Cam's indifference increased. She no longer wanted the money just for its own sake, but as of proof of his love.

He refuses to make a will! He pointed out that if he dies intestate I am automatically his heir. Yet he knows I am older than he and might never inherit – and what about my little Muriel. I will not allow him to get away with this. I must make her secure.

But it was too late. Cam knew now that Margaret had married him for his money; in an unguarded moment she had told him she would never have left the man she was living with but for the promise of a better deal. Sickened and disillusioned, he turned away from her and remained deaf to all her pleas for financial independence. He reiterated that she could have what she wanted for herself, the house, the child, but he paid the bills and he would not give her money.

Margaret's demands for money and attention began to sicken him. She used every means she could to attract and reawaken his interest in her physically, but he drew further and further away. Perhaps if she had let him alone things might have been different, but her blatant attempts to entice him without subtlety revealed to me – the reader of her diary – her basically coarse approach to life. Knowing Cam's fastidiousness, his idealistic and romantic attitude to love, how easily I could understand his aversion to such a woman. She had been taught her lessons in loving by the worthless man she had run off with. She reverted now to those days in a last desperate effort to seduce Cam. He locked his door against her.

Margaret's love, if ever it deserved the name, changed to hate. She began again her incessant pestering for financial independence. It became an obsession. The closely written pages were filled with new schemes, new ideas for persuading Cam that he must make a will in her or Muriel's favour. Once she almost succeeded, by continuous nagging, in persuading him to see his lawyer. But some weeks later the diary was scored across in huge dark lines with one word: FAILED! At the last minute Cam had not kept the appointment.

The tone of the diary changed again. The violent hatred that followed the thwarted love now turned to self-pity. What was to become of her? What was to become of the child? Suppose Cam were to fall in love with someone else and leave her? Could she be sure of a third of his income if it came to a divorce? What *was* his income? She had no doubt he was rich, but how rich? Suppose he had no capital? She knew nothing of his assets except his ownership of this great useless house full of antiques. She began to see she was unlikely now to obtain a will in her favour, but was determined to see her child was made financially secure.

She began a new onslaught upon Cam to adopt the child by law, knowing that only if Muriel bore his name would she legally inherit if Cam died. Again Cam refused. He promised to care for Muriel for as long as was necessary and regardless of any future events, but he would not give his name to another man's child. In his view it wasn't necessary since Muriel was legitimate and had a father, albeit one Margaret had divorced long ago for desertion and had not seen since.

Margaret went on trying. Week after week, month after month, she filled the pages of the diary with accounts of her fruitless efforts to make herself or her child Cam's legal heir. Cam's reply was always the same: '*Without the existence of a will, you are already my heir*'.

But now Margaret began to doubt again. '*How,*' she wrote, '*can I be sure he hasn't made a will in someone else's favour?*'. Maybe he had living relatives of whom she was unaware. Maybe he had a woman somewhere, kept by him the way she herself had once been kept. How did she know who Cam kept in the London flat where he now spent so much of his time?

The thought that she or Muriel might not get Cam's money was bad enough, but that someone else might inherit was unbearable. She thought of little else. Bouts of bitter recrimination were followed by deep depressions. The fact that she was now living in the lap of luxury, that she and her child lacked nothing in the world they wanted, that she was socially secure and her position invulnerable if she behaved in a reasonable fashion, did not seem to console her. The depression increased. Cam was obviously concerned about her, for she mentioned in the diary not more than a month before her death that he was trying to persuade her to see a doctor. He even stifled his own feelings sufficiently to suggest she leave Quarry House and go to London with him for a holiday.

'To cheer me up!' she wrote bitterly. '*When all the time he knows only too well how to make me happy. Hypocrite!*'

There were a few more entries, each one more depressive, with occasional bursts of vindictiveness.

'I'll make him pay for the way I suffer! I'll make him sorry. My poor, poor baby! My poor little Muriel!'

I drew a deep, shuddering sigh. No wonder my darling Cam clung to me with such tenacity. He had never talked about those years with Margaret, and I doubt if I would have understood the full horror of them if I hadn't read this document. I was filled with pity for him – for the poor wretched woman, too, though it was obvious to me that she was the victim of her own greed. A woman who marries for money does not really deserve pity – yet I pitied her.

I pitied Cam, too, for all those wasted years. And I pitied the little girl who had absorbed her mother's pathetic outpourings and learned to hate the man whom she called her father. I thought that at last I understood why Muriel had tried to turn me against Cam, inventing any story she could think of likely to cause a rift between us. She did not hate me, but she did not want me to make Cam happy by continuing to love him.

Impulsively, I went straight back to the studio, not by the dark secret passage, but across the courtyard. I was no longer afraid. I knew I could cope with anything now that I understood Muriel's behaviour and motives.

I had forgotten that Logan might still be in the studio, but apparently he had not stayed long after I left. Muriel was alone. I handed the diary back to her. Words came easily to me now.

'You must try not to blame your stepfather for your mother's unhappiness,' I said gently. 'He tried to do the best he could. He was no more responsible for the failure of the marriage than your mother. Many marriages fail on the grounds of incompatibility, and it would be wrong to apportion blame. Try not to feel bitter, Muriel. Try to forget the past.'

Muriel's voice startled me by its violence.

'Forget?' she said in a small hard voice. 'When anyone can see he drove my mother to her death just as surely as if he'd killed her! Haven't you realised yet what kind of man you married?'

Unknowingly, I drew back from her, shivering. 'Muriel, *no*!' I said violently. 'There was a time when Cam truly believed he loved her. You cannot blame him because she had tricked him into marriage, pretending she loved him.'

Muriel's eyes were hard. 'Love? What does *that* matter?' she cried. 'He hadn't the common decency to make her secure – a woman who'd been poor all her life and wanted security. It wasn't so much to ask, was it? He refused, and I know why – to punish her.'

'No. Muriel, *no*!' I burst out. 'That isn't like Cam – you know in your heart that it isn't like him. Whatever his reasons for refusal they were not vindictive – that I'll swear.'

'Oh, you!' Muriel spat out the words scornfully. 'You're so besotted with him you can't see the truth any more than Jennifer could. She was just like you – stupid, trusting, thinking he was marvellous. He drove my mother to her death – that's the truth.'

I remained silent. Muriel had lived with the diary since the age of twelve – an age when she could not possibly have understood all the implications. Her judgment was that of a child, and moreover the partisan judgment of a child for its mother. She had come by this diary at a stage of adolescence when it could most work its evil upon her. I bitterly condemned the woman who could have left it for a twelve-year-old to read.

Now the fire seemed to have gone out of Muriel. When she spoke to me again it was with that old casual tone which I found so unnerving. 'Logan is the only one besides myself to see facts,' she said, as much to herself as to me. '*He* knows. He's the only other one to recognise my mother's real murderer!'

Anger welled up in me. 'Don't ever use that word in front of me again, Muriel!' I said with such intensity that even she raised her eyebrows in surprise. 'If Logan has encouraged that idea, then the less you see of him in future the better. The only possible excuse for either of you is that you were so young when it all happened. But you are adult now, Muriel, and if you truly believe what you say, how do you explain the fact that you are still living here under Cam's roof? Accepting his protection? Taking money from him? Calling him Father and pretending an affection for him?'

Muriel gave a short hard laugh. 'Don't think I *want* to live here, Kate. If you imagine that you are even more stupid than I believed. I stay because I know he'd *like* to get rid of me. I won't give him that satisfaction.'

She walked back to the curtain, drawing it once more away from the painted canvases. 'Look! See how I resemble my mother. Just think how much I must remind him of her. He thought he'd got off scot-free when the verdict was suicide. He thought he'd be able to forget she ever existed. But he can't, can he, so long as I'm around?'

I felt frightened by the malice and hatred in her voice. I said, 'Cam could turn you out if he wanted, Muriel. If the sight of you really made him feel unhappy or guilty, he *would* have turned you out long ago, wouldn't he?'

'No! His conscience won't let him. You forget he swore to my mother he'd take care of me no matter what happened. And then there are the children; he relies on me to look after them.'

'Not any more, Muriel. I'm here now.'

She shrugged as if she knew perfectly well that I presented no danger. 'You probably won't be here long,' she said in a matter-of-fact voice.

'I'm not sure what gives you that idea, Muriel. I shall be here all the holidays, every holiday.'

'Until you follow in Jennifer's footsteps!'

The moment of anger I felt quickly gave way to helplessness. I was, after all, no nearer understanding Muriel or her motives. For a brief while, I had believed her misguided but sane. Now I was forced once more to question the state of her mind.

'You'll die – just the way Jennifer did. She wouldn't listen to me either!' Muriel said, sighing. And added illogically, 'Don't say I didn't warn you!'

If she intended to frighten me as to my own safety, she failed, but she did succeed in frightening me for Cam.

When I left Muriel and returned to the house, I found Cam. I insisted on talking to him about Muriel's mental state. I would not let him laugh it off this time as hysterical nonsense. It wasn't and I knew it wasn't.

But to my intense dismay, Cam refused to take any action. He listened because I made him do so. I warned him that I would walk straight out of the house and never come back if he did not. I told him then that I had read the diary and of the conversation that ensued. His face remained impassive and he did not try to interrupt me. When I finally came to a full stop, he looked at me almost pityingly. 'I suppose it is natural you should be shocked. But it comes as no surprise to me, Kate. You see, I've been through all this once before. Muriel tried to poison Jennifer's mind against me, just as she is now trying to poison yours. Fortunately Jennifer took it a lot more calmly than you are doing. She was a very placid person, and I suppose it all struck her as so ridiculous she never gave it serious thought.'

Was there a hint of reproof in Cam's voice – as if he wished I could react like Jennifer? But I couldn't.

'Muriel is mentally ill!' I cried. 'If nothing else, you must agree we should do something about that.'

'I don't think she is mental – only irrational about her mother's death. I'm not anxious to stir up the past, Kate. It was a wretched period of my life, and I prefer to forget it. If you could only bring yourself to ignore her, she's quite harmless.'

Another reproof? The protest died on my lips. I could understand how much Cam wanted to put those years right out of his mind. I, too, would like to, but the diary was still too fresh in my memory.

'Kate, darling, it's the future that matters – you and me and our life,' he said, taking me in his arms and holding me fiercely. 'You swore you didn't care that I'd been married before, that it wouldn't make any difference that you were my third wife. But it *is* making a difference. You're letting the past come between us!'

'No, darling, no!' I cried, so vehemently that I almost but not quite convinced myself as well as Cam.

'Then forget Muriel!' Cam said violently. 'Forget her and her crazy ideas and treat them with the contempt they deserve.'

It was certainly the easiest solution and weakly I acquiesced. But only half my will lay behind the effort. One part of me told me it was wrong to ignore this. Muriel needed a doctor's care. When anything preyed on a person's mind the way her mother's suicide preyed on Muriel's, the effect could be serious.

I comforted myself with the thought that, though new to me, this situation had existed for six years. If Muriel's mind were to break under the strain, it would surely have done so long before now.

We returned to London where my relationship with Cam improved at once. He was indisputably happiest when he had me completely to himself. Muriel could be pushed to the back of my mind, and Cam himself gave no cause for anxiety. I began to think that the caution Robert had advised so strongly in his letter was out of proportion to the facts and blamed myself for having written in such a way as to have given him a false impression of Cam. Cam was gentle, loving, attentive, lover-like. This month in London was the happiest we had ever spent together. We had never been closer to one another than we were then.

For this reason, I dreaded a return to Quarry House and yet looked forward to it. I was quite unreasonably excited by the anticipation of seeing the little girls again and by the thought of the pleasure and happiness I would be giving them this Christmas. I wanted to make it a memorable occasion for Cam and the children.

I would have liked to give a children's party, too, but we had no neighbours at Quarry House, and Cam was against the idea of giving a party for the village children.

'They wouldn't come!' he told me, his face dark and unhappy. 'It's the old story, Kate – their parents have gossiped too much about the mysterious "goings on" at the Big House. I'm sorry!'

'Perhaps we could have some of the girls' school friends to stay?' I temporised. But Cam thought this was unnecessary – they would see enough of their friends at school.

'Isn't there anyone we can invite to share our happiness?' I asked. I suppose my voice must have sounded wistful for Cam put his arms round me and said, 'I'm afraid you've married a man who doesn't have many friends. I used to feel lonely up in Yorkshire but it all changed when you came. Now I don't want anyone else – only you. If I have you, I have everything in the world I want.'

But later, lying in the darkness in Cam's arms, I felt a renewed sadness that I lived in a 'haunted' house where no child wanted to come. The past could not be entirely forgotten after all.

Chapter Thirteen

I suppose it was inevitable that I should see Robert again at Christmas. I was frequently down in the village, buying groceries for Mrs Meadows or paper chains for the children or helping them with their own present-buying. We were busy mailing Christmas cards to their school friends when we ran into Robert.

We had not been in touch since our exchange of letters about Cam, and I think we were both a little embarrassed. Robert shook my hand, saying 'How lovely to see you!' twice before he realised he had not let go. He dropped it quickly and self-consciously.

We exchanged trivial gossip while the children jumped around him, obviously pleased to see him. Lillian, the youngest and the least inhibited, clung to his arm, her face pink with excitement.

'We've got an absolutely *fabulous* tree!' she said, opening her short arms as wide as they would go. 'It's all covered in *things*. You'll come and see it, won't you, Dr Carnes?'

Sandra and Debbie seconded Lillian's invitation.

I could see Robert looking at me hesitantly. I didn't know what to say. My first instinct was to add my pleas to the children's, but what of Cam? Would he mind? Surely not at Christmas, I thought, trying to make myself believe he would act normally now our relationship was so secure.

I spoke lightly, smiling at Robert with an assumed casualness. 'I'll give you a ring and fix a date, shall I?' I prevaricated. This would give me time to ask Cam first. He was in such a happy frame of mind I didn't want to spoil the perfection of this first week of the holidays – not even for Robert. But I didn't like to think of the lonely Christmas the young doctor would probably have. Cam couldn't in all conscience refuse to ask him up for a drink even if he didn't want to invite Robert to join us for family lunch.

I was beginning to learn the real meaning of tact. I meant to choose the right moment to ask Cam when we were alone. But the minute the children and I got back to Quarry House, they rushed over to Cam all talking at once. He was standing on top of the step-ladder fixing holly over the hall mirror when the girls burst out with the news that they'd seen Dr Carnes and that he was coming to look at the tree.

'It'll b-b-be the most b-beautiful tree he's ever seen!' said Sandra, eyes glowing, her stammer so much better since she'd been away at school.

'But we've got to put a *present* on for him!' Lillian cried. 'Everyone else has got one so he must have one, too, mustn't he, Daddy?'

I prayed silently that Cam would say nothing to spoil this spontaneous rush of Christian goodwill in his children. I felt him staring at me and I looked up at him steadily. 'We met in the post office when we were mailing our cards,' I said with far more calm than I felt. 'The children invited him to come and see our tree. I told him I'd ring up and fix it. What do you think, darling? Shall we ask him up?'

'Do what you think best!' Cam replied. But there was no answering smile and he turned his head away from me. Despite the reasonableness of his words and tone, I felt uneasy.

'Tell him to come *today* –' Lillian chattered on innocently. 'I want him to come now. May I turn the tree lights on, Kate? May I?'

'There's no hurry, Lillian!' I said. 'There are still three days to Christmas. I think we'll wait till Christmas Eve and perhaps invite Dr Carnes then.'

I hoped this would let Cam know that I personally was in no hurry to see Robert.

The subject was not raised again. Several times I was on the point of bringing it up, but I didn't. Everything was going so well that I couldn't risk upsetting the happy warm atmosphere in the house.

Even Muriel seemed to be making an effort to be pleasant to everyone. She added her own presents to ours by the tree. They were carefully and beautifully wrapped in gold paper.

I helped Mrs Meadows to prepare a mountain of good food for the festivities. She and old Meadows would be eating Christmas lunch at the house, so there were eight to feed. The kitchen was filled with steamy heat and the delicious smell of baking. Lights shone everywhere, and the house looked golden, sparkling, and colourful. It was going to be a real family Christmas just as I had imagined. I was very happy.

Cam, too, must have caught the carefree atmosphere. He raised no objection when the day of Christmas Eve came and I told him I was going to telephone Robert that morning. I hoped that once Cam got to know Robert a little better – talked to him over drinks – he would begin to like him and might even accept him as a friend. If all went well, I could ask Robert to stay on after drinks and have a meal with us.

I didn't realise how nervous I was when evening approached and I was setting out the drinks on the sideboard. Cam was upstairs changing. It took Muriel's penetrating eye to notice that my hands were trembling as I set out the glasses. To my acute annoyance, I blushed like a silly schoolgirl when she remarked upon it.

'Don't be stupid, Muriel,' I snapped. 'Why should I be nervous?'

But she had succeeded in making me doubly so.

When the doorbell rang, it was Muriel who went to answer it. Cam had still not appeared. When Muriel brought Robert into the drawing-room, I asked her to go and tell Cam our guest had arrived.

'Please help yourself to a drink, Robert,' I said. 'Cam will be down in a minute.'

'That's okay, I'll wait,' Robert said. 'Or would you like one now?'

I shook my head. My voice seemed to have deserted me. Muriel did not return, and I was consumed with a terrible anxiety that Cam was never going to appear. I couldn't concentrate on making conversation. It was therefore a relief to both of us when the little girls came running in to greet Robert. They all talked at once and succeeded in dragging him out to the hall to take a proper look at the tree. Sandra paused in the doorway. 'M-may we g-give him his present now, Kate? Please can we?'

I nodded. We'd bought a bottle of sherry for Robert. There was still no sign of Cam. While Robert was in the hall with the girls opening his parcel, I took the opportunity to hurry upstairs to our room in search of my husband.

Cam was fully dressed, standing by the window smoking. I stood in the doorway staring at him. 'Darling, Robert's here,' I said. 'Didn't Muriel tell you?'

Cam's face was expressionless, but his voice was hard as he replied. 'Yes, she told me. But I'm in no great hurry to greet your boyfriend.'

Not again, I thought! Please, God, don't let Cam do this to me again. My first reaction was of fear, but I stifled it. I went across to him and put my arms round him. 'My boyfriend, as you call him, may think it a little odd if his host doesn't appear!' I said as casually as I could. 'You do look nice, Cam. I love that suit. It makes you look very distinguished.'

Suddenly, he grabbed hold of me and held me at arm's length.

'And you look bloody beautiful!' he said violently. 'For him, I suppose! No doubt he's been appreciating it!'

We were on the verge of a terrible row. As if in a nightmare, I felt I was being inexorably drawn toward disaster. This was what I had subconsciously been dreading all evening. But I refused to go under. I mustered all my self-control and acted as if Cam's behaviour was perfectly reasonable.

'I couldn't tell you if Robert appreciates my appearance or not!' I said with a forced laugh. 'Nor do I care. All I can tell you is that he won't have a drink until you come down, so I think we'd better go and do our duty to our guest, don't you?'

I could feel the tension in Cam, running along his arms, and into my shoulders; his fingers were digging into my flesh, hurting me.

'*Your* guest!' he corrected me, eyes narrowed and brilliant. '*My* guest then!' I agreed. 'Come on, darling. We can't leave him to the children indefinitely.'

Again I felt that hesitation as if the two sides of Cam's nature were warring with each other. I was sure that if I could continue to stay calm, I would win this battle. I said gaily, 'Very well, I'm ready, darling, if you are.'

As he let go of me, I let out my breath. It was all right. I had won. I hid my feelings of elation. Cam's face was still stiff and expressionless. He was fighting hard to keep himself in control. He followed me downstairs. As we went into the drawing-room, I deliberately linked my arm through his. I saw Robert look at us, caught a glimpse of the anxiety in his face that was quickly replaced with relief. He, too, had been worried!

It was Robert who carried the three of us through the next five minutes with small talk, chatting easily to Cam about the previous occasion on which they had met prior to our marriage, about the busy time he was having before Christmas with the surgery full. He deliberately did not look at me or speak to me. I was grateful.

'The surgery will be quite different tomorrow and during the holiday!' Robert said with that pleasant, easy smile. 'All of a sudden, no one will feel ill – all too busy enjoying themselves eating Christmas dinner to waste time with imaginary aches and pains!'

Cam did not comment, but he dispensed a second round of drinks and we sat down, Cam and I on the sofa, Robert opposite. Cam made no effort to contribute to the conversation but he did at least reply, if briefly, to Robert's questions. Yes, he'd been pretty busy at the office. Yes, it was nice to be home for Christmas. No, the children did not know what they were getting for Christmas. He was coldly polite but quite unbending.

Naturally enough, Robert eventually turned his conversation towards me. I, too, was conscious of the awfulness of the silence that threatened to fall. I responded eagerly, talking too much in my nervousness. Most of what I said was complete nonsense. Cam's unblinking gaze made me feel hopelessly self-conscious. My hand shook, and I found myself trying to look past Robert as I spoke to him, in case Cam should think I was looking at him with hidden meaning.

It was so ridiculous that I could have wept. Nothing could alter the way the atmosphere was developing – Cam silent, me talking rubbish, and Robert doing his best to make sense of what I said and trying to help me out with suitable replies.

It was an enormous relief when Robert stood up saying he must go; he still had a lot of work to do. I knew it was a lie because he had told me on his arrival that he'd finally cleared his desk before the holiday and was free now to enjoy himself.

I was silent at last. I could not bring myself to utter the conventional 'But must you go so soon!'. Robert could not possibly be enjoying himself, nor, indeed, was I. I was so upset I no longer cared what Cam thought. I said deliberately, '*I'll* show you out, Robert!'

It was an act of defiance. I think I half expected Cam to try to stop me, but he didn't. He merely nodded a formal goodnight to Robert. As we left the room, I saw him walk over to the sideboard to pour himself another drink.

The hall was empty. The Christmas tree still blazed with light. I thought suddenly how artificial the tinsel looked and how meaningless those mysterious parcels which until now had seemed so exciting. I bent and picked up the bottle of sherry Robert had left at the foot of the tree and gave it to him.

'I'm sorry!' I said. 'I didn't think it would be like that. I'm so sorry, Robert. What a start to Christmas!'

There were tears at the back of my eyes and I closed them quickly. I didn't want Robert to see how upset I was. I felt his hand on mine – a warm, strong reassuring grasp.

'Forget it, Kate. Do you understand? Forget it. Have a happy Christmas. I mean that. Don't lose heart.'

I gulped, his sympathy and understanding nearly undermining my intention not to cry like a child whose party had been spoiled.

I watched him as he put on his overcoat and walked to the front door. He turned and looked at me. I was still standing by the tree. He smiled. I felt a sudden longing to rush over to him and beg him not to go. Not to leave me here alone in this house with Cam – a man who had become a stranger to me, a man I was actually afraid of now. Robert represented solidity, normality, safety. *I didn't want him to go.*

Then the door closed behind him and I heard his car start up noisily in the drive. I waited until the sound of the engine died away down the hill and then let out my breath. Slowly, I bent down to switch off the tree lights. I picked up the coloured wrapping paper and folded it carefully into a neat square. I straightened a piece of holly and carefully lifted a fallen scarlet berry from the carpet. There was nothing more to do.

Then I caught my breath. I saw Cam standing in the drawing-room doorway, silhouetted against the background of lights. How long he had been there watching me I didn't know. I heard him laugh.

'Poor devil!' he said in a strange harsh voice. 'Must have been a pretty frustrating sort of evening for him...didn't even have a chance to kiss you under the mistletoe!'

'Cam...' I began, but he did not give me a chance to complete my sentence. He covered the distance between us in two great strides.

'Never mind, Kate!' he said, gripping my upper arms and forcing me close up against him. 'I'll kiss you for him, shall I, like this?'

If it is possible to assault someone with a kiss, then Cam assaulted me. I fought him with all the strength I had, as immune as he to the fact that at any moment Mrs Meadows or one of the children might come by. But my efforts to escape from him only increased the intensity of his emotions.

When at last he drew his mouth away, it was to say, 'You belong to me, Kate. Do you hear? You're mine and no one else is ever going to have you. *Mine, mine mine!*'

I held my hands against my bruised lips and saw blood. I was shivering so violently that my teeth chattered. 'You hurt me!' I cried, trying to release myself from his grasp. 'Let me go. You *hurt* me!'

'I'll never let you go, Kate, not as long as I live!'

I flung back my head and stared up at him furiously. 'If you ever do anything like that again, I'll leave you, Cam. I swear it. Now let me go.'

I don't think he even heard me. I'm sure he would not have released me but for the opportune arrival of Mrs Meadows. 'Supper's ready,' she said brightly. 'Shall I dish it up now?'

Cam's hands fell to his sides. He gave Mrs Meadows an odd little smile. 'By all means, let's eat,' he said.

I had only a glimpse of Mrs Meadows' eyes gazing anxiously at me before Cam tucked his arm into mine and forcibly drew me into the dining-room, where the rest of the family sat waiting for their meal.

Chapter Fourteen

For the sake of the little girls, I made a supreme effort to be cheerful over Christmas. But apart from my misgivings about my marriage, I was not feeling at all well. I put down my constant feeling of nausea to too much rich food and lack of sleep. Cam had had what I now was beginning to recognise as his usual reaction to the scene about Robert. His remorse and pleas for forgiveness I found almost as difficult to cope with as the scene itself. I didn't like to see him humble himself so totally; nor hear him beg my forgiveness.

But at least the little girls were happy. The gifts I had chosen for them were a complete success. Many were occupational, so they were kept busy in the nursery with paints and puzzles and the little miniature sewing machines I had found for them.

Cam, and I were outwardly reconciled. He seemed his normal self and over-solicitous about my health. Muriel spent a great deal of time in her studio, often with Logan for company. I did not know if she was glad to have more time for her painting, but I insisted upon taking full charge of the three girls myself, regardless of her wishes. Although Cam would not agree that Muriel was bad for them, he didn't raise any objection. Since Muriel seemed not to care one way or the other, my takeover went smoothly enough.

Cam, still remorseful after the scene on Christmas Eve, was pathetically anxious to do anything he could to please me. He was constantly at my side.

The nursery became my escape from his over-possessiveness. I knew that he kept a close watch on everything I did and everywhere I went. Although I had absolutely nothing whatever to conceal from him, nor ever had, his brooding attentiveness made me feel like a prisoner on parole. It was only when I was actually in his company or with the girls that he seemed to relax and be his former, contented untroubled self.

Robert's name was never mentioned – at least not between Cam and me. I did, however, overhear a conversation between Muriel and Logan which annoyed and distressed me. I lifted the upstairs extension of the telephone to make a call to the village as I had some groceries to order. I should have replaced the receiver the moment I heard Muriel speaking on the downstairs phone but, hearing my own name, I was silly enough and weak enough to do something quite foreign to my normal behaviour; I listened in.

'...and if Kate sees Robert Carnes again, I wouldn't like to answer for the consequences. Father is convinced she's attracted to him and you can understand why. He is nice-looking and much nearer her age than Father.'

I felt slightly sick at Logan's responding snigger. But I continued listening as he said in his effeminate voice, 'Don't see what you can do about the situation, old girl. She's not your responsibility. It's up to her if she wants to take risks.'

Muriel might have been in the same room so clearly did her sigh sound in my ear. 'I've tried to warn her. I even showed her the diary. It didn't make any difference – she won't let me say a word against Father. One would hardly credit anyone being so silly – but that's the way she is. She reminds me of poor Jennifer. She'd never listen to me, either.' She gave a sarcastic little laugh which made me want to rush downstairs and hit her. 'Kate has forbidden me to say one word against "the man she loves". Love! What does she know about it. Moonlight and roses! That's her version. She hasn't the capacity to love the way my mother did.'

'Well, you can't do more than warn her!' Logan said, sounding a trifle bored. I imagined he'd heard Muriel on the subject of her mother many times before and was cutting her short. 'Want me to have a word with her?'

'I don't think it would help, Logan. She doesn't like you. Anyway, she'd be sure to think I'd put you up to it. I'll just have to find a suitable opportunity to have another try. Let's hope it won't be too late. Frankly, I don't much like the way things are going. If you ask me, the marriage is beginning to crack already. Father won't let her out of his sight. He doesn't trust her.'

I finally managed to put down the receiver. I was trembling with a mixture of anger and nausea. That an eighteen-year-old girl should discuss Cam and me in such a manner with anyone – let alone a weak layabout like Logan – revolted me. I longed to go and tell Cam that he must finally come to grips with his stepdaughter. I simply couldn't understand why he was so unwilling to send her away, or at least try to persuade her to leave. She was a troublemaker. Although I felt sorry for her and could appreciate that Cam felt he owed her a great deal for her care of his other children in the past, the fact was we would all be a great deal happier if she did not live at Quarry House.

But my first impulsive desire to tell Cam what I'd overheard soon dimmed when I realised it would be a useless quest. I couldn't mention Muriel's remarks about Robert and myself since he'd probably agree with them.

And if I were merely to say I disliked her, he would remind me that this was Muriel's home as well as mine. Though it was true that Cam's first allegiance now was to me, his wife, and that I was mistress of Quarry House, I was not prepared to go to the lengths of giving him an ultimatum – Muriel goes or I go. I hoped without any conviction that time would solve the problem: that Muriel might leave of her own free will, or alternatively that Cam would see for himself how disrupting an influence she was.

But Muriel was no fool. Outwardly, she was always polite and helpful, especially if Cam were within earshot. She was never obtrusive and in the evenings, when the younger ones were safely tucked up in bed, Muriel would leave Cam and me alone together after our evening meal, disappearing to the studio or to her bedroom. Logan was a frequent visitor but he, too, kept out of the way, for which I was grateful. As for myself, I quite openly and deliberately avoided them both.

A week passed, and the old year gave way to the new. Cam went back to the office for five days without me. No matter how hard he pleaded, I would not go with him; partly because I didn't feel up to the journey, but most of all because I refused to leave the little girls alone in Muriel's charge.

'I know they're not my children, Cam, but I love them. I couldn't go away with a clear conscience while they're home for their holidays, and that's all there is to it.'

'Then you don't really love me...' Cam began, but even he was silenced by the look on my face.

His own was so unbearably miserable when he left on Sunday evening, I nearly relented. He needed me and I loved him. I wondered if my duty as a wife should override my fears for the children who were not even my own flesh and blood. In the end, my health decided the issue for me – I just didn't feel up to the journey.

It was Mrs Meadows who first put the idea in my head that I might be pregnant. I couldn't hide my dismay when she first asked me with a countrywoman's directness, if I might not be carrying a child.

'And what's so terrible if you are?' she asked me, seeing my face. 'Do us all a power of good to have another little one in the nursery. And if it is to be, make sure it's a boy this time!'

I ran to the seclusion of my room. *I didn't want a baby.* I couldn't cope with one on top of everything else. I counted up the weeks and rushed down to Robert's surgery.

He questioned me closely, spoke to me calmly, soothingly, and suggested a test that could speedily determine the facts.

'We'll know in twenty-four hours,' he told me. 'Then you can put your mind at rest. I gather you don't want a baby by the way you've been carrying on. I'd have expected you to be pleased, Kate.'

Until that moment, sitting there in Robert's shabby room with the coal fire in the little black grate and his books filling every shelf and table space, I had not realised the extent of the control I had been exerting upon myself. I cried for five minutes. Then my worries poured out of me like water from a broken dam.

'I'm just not able to deal with Cam or Muriel!' I ended, still tearful. 'I can't cope – that's the truth of the matter, and with a baby on top of everything else...'

Robert looked at me across the desk, eyes sympathetic and concerned. 'But you still love your husband, don't you?'

'Yes, *of course!*' I said without hesitation. Of this much at least I was sure.

'Then stop worrying, Kate. In the first place, there may be no baby. The sickness, all your symptoms...could be caused by nerves. As for Campbell...don't you think you possibly *could* persuade him, for the sake of your marriage, to see a psychiatrist or another doctor? Obviously he won't let me try to help him.'

I shivered. 'I doubt it. Cam knows very well how he upsets me but I don't honestly think he is aware how irrational his behaviour is. Tell me, Robert, could things get better? Or must they get worse? Can't one ever get the better of jealousy? Surely in time Cam will learn to trust me.'

If Robert knew the answer, he did not intend to tell me. He said more to himself than to me, 'I just wish there were someone else in that house with you other than old Meadows.'

I began to recover my equilibrium and hastened to correct any false impression I'd given Robert about Cam.

'If you're thinking I'm in any kind of danger, Robert, I must have exaggerated terribly. Of course Cam wouldn't *hurt* me. That's just Muriel's nonsense. I never took her warning seriously. Cam loves me.'

Robert nodded, but disconcertingly stubborn, he said, 'Love and hate are never so very far apart in our emotions, Kate. No matter how much you may try to whitewash it, Cam has shown violence on several occasions.'

I nearly smiled. 'You're beginning to sound like Muriel,' I said. 'You'll be trying to warn me I'm third on the list of Cam's wives to be disposed of!' I did laugh now, a trifle hysterically. But Robert remained serious.

'Tell me again exactly what Muriel has been saying, Kate,' he urged me.

I told him about the diary, about Muriel's phone call to Logan. I told him how Cam had shrugged off the diary and its horrible implications. 'He wouldn't take it seriously and maybe he's right,' I ended. 'I honestly don't know any more, Robert. To tell you the truth, I'm almost beginning to doubt my own sanity.'

Robert leaned forward on his elbows, his face thoughtful. 'You may think I have been poking my nose too far into your private affairs,' he said. 'But I think it may help you to know something I've discovered. I went to the trouble to look up the account of the inquests on the deaths of both Margaret and Jennifer Rivers. There was quite definitely a suicide note in the first instance, and your husband was in London at the time of Jennifer's death. At least, he said so, and he certainly wasn't at Quarry House. Cam's innocence is unquestionable despite any gossip you might have heard to the contrary and despite anything Muriel may try to make you believe.'

'But how did all those ugly rumours begin,' I asked, 'if there was never the slightest suspicion of Cam being responsible? It's so unfair!'

Robert hesitated. 'There *was* an anonymous letter sent to the magistrate. It pointed out that there was no alibi for Cam Rivers and that he could well have driven from London to Yorkshire, murdered Jennifer, and driven back again. In such an isolated part of the world, his car would not necessarily have been seen.'

'But who could have written such a thing...' I broke off as the truth struck me. 'Muriel?' I whispered.

'Could have been. It was written in an educated script. But the police never did find out who sent the letter, and in view of the fact that it was anonymous, it was disregarded in court. Cam was completely cleared, and the court expressed its sympathy.'

Once again I shivered. 'All Muriel's implications suggest I am to be number three victim,' I said with an attempt to be jocular. 'If I'm not careful, Robert, I shall start believing it myself, especially with you telling me I need a bodyguard.'

I wanted Robert to laugh and say 'Rubbish' and to tell me I was being imaginative and silly. But he said nothing.

'You'd better give me a bottle of something which will help me to pull myself together,' I said stupidly.

I half hoped he would suggest some pep pills or tranquillisers. I needed something! But I only got more advice.

'The moment Cam gets back from London, you must tell him you've been to see me,' he said, 'If you don't, Muriel might try to make more trouble by telling him before you do. I'll phone you as soon as I have the result of the test. Meanwhile, try not to worry. Spend as much time as possible with those nice kids. I'm sure they're good for you. What a little enchantress young Lillian is! I wish I could see more of the girls myself.'

'I do, too!'

We had both spoken spontaneously. I wondered if he thought as I did what a pity it was we could not be friends as well as neighbours and that he could come to the house assured of a welcome. As things were, I doubted he'd ever want to set foot in my home again! I felt miserable and anxious.

But seeing Robert, pouring out my troubles to him, must have been beneficial in some way, for I had no more nausea. I was not even very surprised – merely relieved – to receive his phone call to tell me the result of the pregnancy test was negative.

Cam came home Friday evening. His greeting was so loving and so intense that I forgot all my worries. We hugged and kissed like a couple of newly-weds.

'I've missed you, darling. I've missed you so much,' he said over and over again.

I don't think we were ever closer to one another than we were for that brief half hour after his arrival. I loved him. I knew that he loved me. He was my husband, my lover, my child. He was all I wanted. Lulled into a false sense of security by the wonderful rapport between us, I spoke without caution or fear. I told him about the scare I had had believing myself pregnant. I could laugh about it now and did so. 'Don't want a baby – just you!' I told him lovingly.

Cam's arms tightened about me. 'How can you be sure you're not pregnant?'

This was the moment when I should have thought carefully before I spoke. But I was not on my guard. I blurted out the truth. I told him I'd been to see Robert, and had had a test which had proved negative.

'So it's quite certain,' I said reassuringly. 'We'll have to be more careful in future, darling. After all, we did take a risk and...'

'You saw Robert Carnes?'

Cam's tone of voice, icy, hard, accusing, was enough warning to bring me quickly back to my senses. I stiffened instantly.

'Of course I went to see Robert, Cam. He is our doctor. *Of course* I had to see him. I felt ill, and I thought I was pregnant. Naturally I went to see him. You understand that, don't you, darling?'

But my attempt to make him approach the subject rationally, logically, was, as always, useless. Cam was on his feet, his face white, eyes narrowed, fists clenched.

'Cam!' I begged. 'Don't, darling, please! You promised you'd never do this again. You *promised*. Can't you see that it's sheer madness? Robert is our doctor. I felt ill and went to the doctor. Think, Cam, *please*.'

I doubt if he heard me. His hands were on my shoulders and he was shaking me. '...could have waited till I came home – alone down there with that man, pawing you...disgusting...any other man's hands so much as touching you...'

The ugly words and insinuations poured out of him. I tried to cover my ears but he wrenched my hands away.

'This time you've gone too far,' he shouted. 'I won't have it...behind my back. I warned you, Kate. There are limits to my patience. You think you can fool me, don't you? Well, you'll find out I can't be cheated so easily. I've suffered enough on your account. Now it's your turn...'

I felt myself growing dizzy as my head rattled to and fro. I knew I must put a stop to this and quickly. Somehow I managed to twist myself out of his grasp. A moment later I opened the bedroom door and ran along the landing and down the stairs. In my panic, I nearly knocked over Muriel, who was standing with her back to the front door. She was smiling. In my confusion I thought she was barring my way. I heard Cam's voice on the upstairs landing calling out to me. 'Kate, stop! Come back, Kate!'

Then Muriel spoke. 'Why don't you use the secret passage?'

Surprise that she was trying to help me escape was quickly followed by renewed fear as Cam began descending the stairs. I turned and ran toward the kitchen, stumbling in the darkness but unwilling to turn on the lights and reveal my whereabouts to Cam. It took me a moment or two to find the stairs to the cellar, and my fear mounted to near hysteria as I tried unsuccessfully to feel for the heavy iron rings of the trapdoor.

I was convinced I could hear footsteps above my head in the kitchen. Frantically, I crawled across the damp cellar floor, hands outstretched until as last I felt the shape of the iron hinges.

My breath came now in quick painful gasps. Only my fear gave me the strength to lift the trapdoor and lower myself into the passage. It was pitch-dark, foul-smelling, and totally unfamiliar. I had to feel my way by placing my outstretched arms against the narrow walls. In my mind, I was certain that the passage had become far longer than when I'd walked along it with Muriel, and that it was leading uphill. It seemed as if I were never going to reach the far end and emerge safely in the harness room.

I was, in fact, perfectly correct in my estimate of the distance between Quarry House and the stable. Somewhere along the tunnel there must have been a branch-off in some other direction, for suddenly, the air began to smell fresher and the cold increased. I could see a faint pale glimmer, which, as I finally emerged into the open, revealed itself as a white frosty moon.

I stared around me in disbelief. I was out of sight of the house, standing on the ledge halfway up the old disused quarry. The temperature was well below freezing. Frantically, I began to scramble up the rocks until I was high up on the hillside. Then only did I pause to draw breath.

It was the intense cold which brought me back to my senses. I was wearing only a thin negligee, and there was a hard frost which I soon became aware of – white and crisp beneath my thin bedroom slippers. I was somewhere on the hill rising up behind Quarry House. Down below me I could see the oblongs of light blazing from the uncurtained windows. I became conscious of hard, jagged rocks around me, and once again, of the biting cold.

I must go back, I thought, I'll freeze to death if I stay out here. I must be out of my mind!

But I stayed still, my breath coming in great gulps, my legs trembling so much I could scarcely stand upright. I tried to rationalise my fear. Cam had been shaking me, beside himself with jealousy and anger. His words still rang in my ears, accusing, threatening:

'...there are limits to my patience. You think you can fool me, don't you? Well, you'll find out that I can 't be cheated

so easily. I've suffered enough on your account. Now it's your turn...'

What had Cam meant? That he intended to hurt me? I had believed so a few minutes ago but now I was beginning to doubt it. Cam loved me. I know he did. He could not have intended to hurt me seriously. He had made no move to strike me – had not lifted a finger, let alone an arm. Why then had I run away? I couldn't *really* be so afraid of my own husband as to rush out into the night half-naked and hide on a hill. That was what I was doing – hiding, trying to shrink back into the dark shadows of the rocks where no one would ever find me.

'Go back! Go back!' the voice of reason demanded. 'You're in far greater danger out here than you ever were indoors.'

A degree of calm began to return – only a degree, but enough to make me pull one of my bedroom slippers onto my cold foot more securely, wrap my thin nylon gown closer about my frozen body. I drew several deep, shuddering breaths and cautiously began to feel my way in the darkness down the hill.

I slipped several times. Small rocks, loosened by my foot, rattled downwards into the black of the night. I stubbed my toe and then fell against a sharp rock and cut my arm. Without knowing it, I began to cry. Now I was becoming stupidly panicky again. I started to think of the past, of Margaret's death on this same hill, of Jennifer, of ghosts. The very house I had run away from began to seem like a haven, a refuge I must reach quickly, or I might die out here alone on the hill.

Then I heard it – the noise. I froze in my descent. At first I thought it was some animal close by – a sheep, perhaps, startled by me and breathing deeply. Then I knew it wasn't an animal but a person. A little to my left I could just discern the dark shape of…a woman? *Or was it a man?*

Cam's name froze on my lips. If it was indeed, Cam, why didn't he call out? Surely he could see me as I could see him. The shadowy outline moved above and behind me. Paralysed into total immobility, I watched as 'it' stopped, lifted something heavy from the ground, and up above my head.

I realised then that someone was going to kill me. Just as in a nightmare, I tried to run and couldn't. I closed my eyes, unwilling to face my approaching death. I heard a shout – unmistakably Cam's voice, and as my eyelids sprang up, a whole world of darkness came rushing towards me. Something hurtled past me. I heard a woman scream – Muriel, I think, and screamed myself.

Suddenly there was silence. Its utter completeness was broken by a low moan from down below me. I could just see a dark shape stretched out across the rocks ten feet or so to my right, below where I stood.

I don't know how I could have been so sure, but I had no doubt at all that it was Cam – and that he was badly hurt. Without thought for my own safety, I slipped and slithered down the distance between us. Stiff with the numbness of frozen limbs, I knelt down beside him. 'Cam! Cam! It's me, Kate!' I don't know why I was whispering.

'Kate? Oh, thank God you are all right!'

I leaned closer to him but as my body touched his, he cried out.

'Are you hurt? Darling, tell me quickly. Are you hurt?'

He seemed to be struggling for breath.

'I'll go and get help!' I cried, trying to keep the panic out of my voice. 'It's all right, Cam. I'll be as quick as I can.'

'No, don't go! Kate, listen to me. *Listen*, Kate. You've *got* to watch out.' His voice was faltering, as if each word were painful to him. 'Are you listening? Muriel – she tried to kill you... I thought I could stop her...she was too quick for me... I slipped. Listen, Kate. Are you listening?'

As gently as I could, I slipped my hand into his. I felt his fingers gripping mine with surprising strength. 'You're to tell Carnes. Do you understand? Tell him...what happened. Tell him he was right. Tell him...' His voice broke off. I waited, holding my breath, for him to continue. Frantically, I withdrew my hand and placed my fingertips on his face. His eyelids were closed. His lips were apart, but I couldn't feel his breath.

'Oh, dear God, no, no!' I prayed silently. 'Don't let him be badly hurt. Don't let anything happen to him. I love him. I love him!'

But gradually I realised that I couldn't just sit there hoping for help that wouldn't come. I must do as Cam said. I'd get Robert.

Only then did the full impact of Cam's words hit me. It must have been Muriel behind me, intending to kill me. Somehow Cam had prevented her. In the darkness he had slipped. But where was Muriel now? Was she still lurking somewhere in the blackness, waiting for another chance to kill me? I had to get back to the house. I had to get help for Cam. If I stayed here I would freeze to death, and so would he.

So I began my faltering journey down the hill. I was so cold now that I couldn't feel my hands or my feet. I fell again and again. If Muriel was hiding, listening for me, she could not have failed to hear me coming. I was sobbing and gasping for breath, praying she would anticipate my returning through the secret passage. I hoped that by taking the longer route down the hillside, I would outwit her.

I reached the drive just as Robert's car turned into it, though I didn't know it was Robert then, and was crazy enough to wonder if the driver was Muriel trying to run me down. I fell on the gravel, badly grazing my legs, arms, elbow and cheek. But I was too cold to feel pain.

The headlights fell full on me where I lay sprawled on the ground. A moment later Robert lifted me up in his arms and carried me into the house.

The next hour is hazy in my memory. I know that Robert wanted me to go to bed, but I wouldn't go. Mrs Meadows bundled me up in warm blankets and I sat in an armchair in the drawing room, shivering. I was made to drink strong tea laced with brandy while Robert disappeared to make some phone calls. My one thought was for Cam, and I couldn't understand why Robert didn't go straight away to look for him.

Later Robert explained to me that if he had gone out alone and found Cam, he couldn't have carried him down the hill unaided. There was also Muriel to be found. He had to telephone for help first.

My next conscious memory was when the men brought Cam back to the waiting ambulance. Robert wouldn't let me see him.

'Campbell's seriously hurt, Kate. I'm taking him to the hospital at once. There's no point you going with him – he's unconscious.'

'But not...not...?'

Robert shook his head.

'No – but it's bad, Kate.'

His face, serious and full of anxiety, was the last thing I saw before I fainted.

When I awoke, the house was silent, Mrs Meadows sat in a chair by my bedside, dozing. I tried to remember what had happened, but the effects of the sleeping pill I'd been given were still too strong for me to think coherently. I closed my eyes and sank back into merciful oblivion.

I woke to find Joanne beside my bed. My head ached fiercely and for a moment, I was unable to co-ordinate my thoughts. Then, gradually I began to remember.

'Cam!' I whispered.

Joanne turned at the sound of my voice, and even in my bemused state, I could interpret the expression on her face. She was regarding me with intense pity. I felt my heart lurch.

She sat down on the side of my bed. 'I'm sorry, darling,' she said gently. 'Cam died a few hours ago. There was nothing they could do to save him.'

I wept, quietly, uncontrollably, in Joanne's arms. When, after a little while, I began to calm down, she sat holding my hand, answering my questions one by one.

When Cam had fallen, he had broken two of his ribs. One had pierced his lung. He had died as the result of a severe haemorrhage soon after Robert and old Meadows had found him. Robert feared the worst but kept the truth from me when they'd brought Cam down from the hillside because he felt I'd had enough shocks for one night without inflicting more.

He telephoned Joanne from the hospital and asked her to come to Quarry House as quickly as possible. She had driven through the night, wanting to be here beside me when I woke.

Strangely, I stopped crying. Perhaps I was still numbed by the after-effect of the sleeping pills. Perhaps I still couldn't believe that Cam, my love, my husband, was really dead: that I would never see him again.

I drank the tea Mrs Meadows brought me and began to question Joanne again. There was so much I still had to know.

'Muriel?' I asked, her name enough to evoke all last night's horror in full.

Joanne's eyes were full of sympathy. She sighed, saying, 'I suppose it will be best if I tell you the whole story. You'll have to know sooner or later. Sure you feel up to it?'

'Yes!' I said vehemently. 'I want to know everything.'

'Well, darling, it seems as if you weren't the only one to believe Muriel was mentally ill. Your young doctor was pretty nearly convinced of it, too. He became seriously worried that day you went to see him when you thought you were pregnant. After what you told him, he thought you might well be in danger; that Muriel could be a psychopath who might already have killed once and be capable of doing so again. Robert felt certain that Cam wouldn't be influenced by your opinion of Muriel, but that he just might be convinced of the potential danger to you if he himself informed him. So he wrote to Cam when he was in London, asking him for your sake, Kate, to get Muriel to a doctor as soon as possible.'

I had had no idea Cam had received such a letter. But then, Cam had only been home a short while before we'd had that terrible row over my visit to Robert's surgery. That was when the whole horrible nightmare of events had begun.

'Obviously, Robert's letter made an impression on Cam,' Joanne continued. 'Maybe Cam had himself suspected Muriel of being abnormal. Maybe he even suspected her of being instrumental in Jennifer's death. Robert said his refusal to admit any such thing was a natural and human reaction. By pushing such thoughts and fears deep into his subconscious, he did not have to act on them. He was probably fighting his dislike of his stepchild, afraid lest he should seem to be prejudiced against her because of his feelings for her mother.'

'But Sandy? Lillian? Debbie?' I cried. 'How could Cam trust *them* to Muriel's care if he secretly believed she...'

'But that's just it!' Joanne broke in. 'He wouldn't *let* himself believe Muriel was sick. Besides, the children never came to any physical harm. Muriel seemed devoted to their care. But they weren't at risk the way you and Jennifer were. You were the ones who had taken the place of Muriel's mother; who were receiving the love she believed Cam had denied her mother.'

Everything Joanne told me was plausible, yet I was still finding it hard to accept.

'I had the impression Muriel liked Jennifer,' I argued. 'I think, in a strange kind of way, she even liked me, silly though she thought me.'

Joanne nodded. 'As I understood it from Robert, it wasn't you or Jennifer Muriel hated. It was Cam, for loving you.'

'And Muriel?' I whispered. 'What has happened to her?' Joanne gave my hand a squeeze. I knew I was not going to like what she had to tell me.

'When Robert and the gardener found Cam on the hill last night, Muriel was sitting there beside him. Her mind had given way completely. Robert said she seemed quite unaware he might be dead. She was talking to him as she must have done many times in her mind, raving at him, telling him how she had killed Jennifer, hoping the blame would fall on him; how angry and frustrated she had been when her anonymous letter to the court had failed to convince anyone of his guilt. She told him she could have killed him many times, but that was not what she wanted. She wanted him imprisoned so that he would spend the rest of his life with nothing else to do but pray for forgiveness for the way he had treated her mother. One day soon, she would succeed in killing you, Kate, making sure that the blame for your death would fall on him.'

Although Joanne's soft voice, telling me these things, bore no relation to Muriel's cold bitter tones, I could almost hear the poor girl's voice. I had once listened to her talking as crazily when she showed me her mother's diary. But uppermost in my mind now was the unbearable thought that Cam had had to listen to her as he lay there dying.

Joanne quickly reassured me. Muriel had run away as soon as she had seen Robert and Meadows approaching. Cam had been barely conscious and would not have understood much of Muriel's ramblings. He had mustered enough strength when he recognised Robert to tell him that he'd been right about Muriel.

I closed my eyes, grief at the thought of Cam's suffering bringing back my tears. Joanne's voice continued. She understood my need to know everything now.

While I had been making my way to the cellar, Muriel had told Cam I had left by the front door. Something odd in her manner had made him doubt her. His jealous anger gave way to a fear for my safety. He recalled Robert's warning and decided to follow her.

It was all becoming clear to me now. Muriel's plan had been a cunning one. She must have overheard the row Cam and I were having and seen the chance to make her move. With me dashing out of the house in my nightclothes and Cam chasing after me, Muriel would have had little difficulty in implicating him had I died that night on the hillside. She had grabbed her opportunity, and only Cam's intervention had saved my life.

I was crying bitterly now. 'He lost his life trying to save me,' I wept.

Joanne tried to calm me. 'His last thoughts were for you, darling. He really did love you. He asked Robert to look after you as best he could.'

I think I was comforted by the knowledge that Cam's jealousy had, at the end, been overcome by his love for me. I was comforted, too, by the assurance Robert gave me some while later that Cam had not died in pain. But for the first few days after Cam's death, I was too numbed with grief and shock to accept comfort. I was aware of only one terrible fact – Cam was dead and I would never see him again.

When I began to feel stronger, Robert called to see me and reluctantly answered my questions. I wanted to know how he had appeared so miraculously in the drive the dreadful night of Cam's death.

He told me that Mrs Meadows had telephoned him to come up to Quarry House after she'd seen Muriel and Cam chasing after me into the night. Understandably, she guessed something terrible was afoot.

'Try not to think about it, Kate,' he said. 'You couldn't have prevented the tragedy. Muriel would have found some way to harm you sooner or later.'

I suppose I should have felt some degree of hate for her, but somehow I couldn't. She had been locked away in a nursing home, her mind completely broken. Robert thought it likely that in due course she would be accused of attempted murder but would probably be considered unfit to stand trial. I was glad, not just for her sake, but for the little girls – and most of all – for Cam. He would so much have hated having his private life and that horrible diary discussed in a public courtroom.

'And Logan?' Joanne asked me what part he had played in this horrible story.

Very little, as it had turned out. He had been entirely under the influence of Muriel. Weak and ineffectual himself, he had merely served as a passive listener to her wild ravings. He had had no hand in Jennifer's death and none in the attempt on my life. The worst that could be said of him was that he had done nothing to discourage Muriel and, by treating her as normal, had given credence to her mad ideas. As I explained to Joanne, he had been friendly with her since early childhood. She probably did not seem insane to him.

I take no credit for the way in which the little girls were protected from the worst of this nightmare ending to the story of my marriage to Cam. Joanne and Mrs Meadows broke the news of their father's death to them. For a few days they were deeply upset and tearful, but their recovery was rapid like most children.

I would not have recovered so quickly myself but for Joanne's wonderful companionship and support in the ensuing weeks. She was more than a mother to me. I leaned on her in so many ways. The formalities of death were new to me, and it was Joanne who organised and coped. Later, she told me that Robert had helped, too, in the background. I saw little of him after the funeral, and then it was time for the girls to return to their boarding schools. Joanne and I went back to London to her flat.

I forgot all about Robert until one evening Joanne told me that he was in love with me. I laughed at the idea and shook my head in denial. I did not want to think about Robert Carnes, far less about love. My marriage to Cam was still too painful and poignant a memory for me to want my emotions disturbed. I was training myself to go about my daily tasks in a shell of immunity that precluded all sentiment. In no other way could I have listened to Cam's lawyers reading me his will, sorted through his papers and clothes, closed the pages of his life. I dared not feel. But Joanne knew that this retreat from life was bad for me. Grief could not be bottled up indefinitely, and the iron control I was imposing on myself was taking its toll. I lost nearly fifteen pounds, and I was nervous and irritable.

I turned to Joanne, my good kind friend, berating her for talking to me about love when my husband was barely three months dead. I told her she was callous and cruel, accused her of having always been prejudiced against my marriage to Cam, of being glad that he had died. I raved at her for nearly ten minutes before finally I broke down and cried as I had not been able to do since the night of Cam's death.

Joanne comforted, forgave, understood. But she would not allow me to withdraw from life indefinitely. It was good for me to be away from Quarry House, and slowly I began to regain a little energy and spirit. As soon as she saw how much better I was, Joanne brought up the subject of Robert again. Again I told her she was being silly to imagine Robert had any special regard for me but I was curious enough to ask her why she should think Robert was in love with me.

'Anyway,' I added, 'Why should he confide in you – a stranger?'

Joanne laughed. 'Hardly a stranger, darling. You weren't well enough to realise what was going on behind your back. Your young doctor and I were in daily touch. He telephoned twice a day for reports on you all the time you were ill. We met in the village, too, on several occasions, to discuss you; needless to say, Robert and I became firm friends. I like him very much.'

'Then it's a pity he hasn't fallen in love with you!' I said flippantly but with a hint of seriousness.

Now it was Joanne who was laughing. 'I hadn't a chance with Robert! It was obvious to me from that very first day I arrived at Quarry House that Robert had only one person on his mind – you. He tried to hide it. How he kept away from the house I just don't know. Fortunately, you weren't in need of medical care. After a few days, he stopped trying to pretend to me that his concern for you was purely that of a doctor. I think he found some relief in telling me how he really felt about you. Seems it was love at first sight though he fought hard against it, knowing how much you loved Cam. He felt he had himself well in control until things started to go wrong between you and Cam, and then all his protective instincts rushed to the fore. Not that he would ever have told anyone, least of all you, how he felt about you so long as you were Cam's wife and his patient. He told me only because he knew he could trust me. He's hoping that given time, you will cease grieving for Cam. Then he means to ask you to marry him.'

'I'll never forget Cam, never!' I cried. 'I really did love him, Joanne. We were so happy. Everything about our marriage was perfect except...'

'I know!' Joanne broke in gently. 'Robert told me about Cam's unreasonable jealousy. You may not see it as yet, darling, but maybe in the end it has all happened for the best. Your marriage could have gone badly wrong if Cam hadn't been able to overcome his fears of losing you. You might even have begun to hate him. Now you can always remember him with love and pride.'

'I couldn't think of marriage to Robert. I don't love him. I don't want any man but Cam!' I protested.

'Of course that's the way you feel now,' Joanne agreed. 'It's right that you should. Robert realised it, and that's why he has said nothing about his love for you. He guessed, too, that you would want to take care of Cam's children and he's perfectly willing to accept them if ever you feel you could marry him. He's quite a man, Kate! I envy you.'

'Even if I loved Robert and wanted to marry him,' I argued, more to put an end to the conversation than because I thought such a thing possible, 'how could he contemplate taking on a wife and three children! He's saving every penny to study for his specialist exams.'

Joanne told me I was now a very rich woman. Cam had set up trust funds for each of the girls, but he had left me all the rest of his capital and Quarry House itself. Joanne forced me to read Cam's will and the lawyer's letter which until now I had refused even to glance at.

'So there's nothing to stop you marrying Robert one day,' Joanne said. 'Money is no problem now.'

'Except that I don't love Robert. I'll never love anyone but Cam. I couldn't love anyone else, Joanne – never!'

Which shows only too clearly the fallibility of human nature.

January gave way to July, and I was packing my suitcase. Tomorrow I was meeting the school train and going down to Quarry House with the children for the summer holidays. I was happy and excited at the prospect, although a part of me dreaded the revival of memories, good and bad. But I knew from their letters the children were eagerly awaiting their return home, and it was time I faced life again with and for them.

'New hairdo?' Joanne asked as she came in from work.

I nodded. 'Like it?'

'Very much!' Joanne said, smiling enigmatically. 'I expect *he* will, too.'

'Don't be ridiculous!' I said crossly. 'You're an incurable romantic, Joanne, but it's no good. I've told you a hundred times I'm not in love with Robert, and I very much doubt if he's still in love with me. He hasn't written for a month, and it's more than likely he's forgotten my existence.'

Still smiling, Joanne reached behind the mirror on the mantelpiece and handed me a letter. 'I was to give it to you today,' she said. 'Mission accomplished.'

I took Robert's letter to my bedroom and there, in the quiet and privacy, I read the most beautiful letter I am ever likely to receive. It ended with this paragraph:

I have tried hard to keep silent, Kate, but now I know I have reached the point where this has become impossible. You will be coming home tomorrow, and my impatient feet will bring me hurrying to your door. When I see you, my dear, dear love, I shall not be able to keep my lips from speaking words of love. I beg you that if they will be unwelcome to you, you telephone me and forbid me to come. If I see you, I know I cannot prevent myself from telling you that I love you; that I want to marry you; that I will wait for years, if need be, if in the end I know you will consent to be my wife.

When I rejoined Joanne, she looked at me questioningly.

'Are you going to telephone him?' she asked.

I shook my head.

Her face showed dismay.

She could not understand – that dear friend of mine – why, at her look of disappointment, I smiled.

CLAIRE LORRIMER

FROST IN THE SUN

Casilda Montero is the beautiful and hot-blooded daughter of a wealthy Spanish aristocrat. Sent from the family hacienda in Southern Spain to an English boarding school, she befriends Joscelin Howard, a shy and serious English girl. Set against the looming tragedy of the Spanish Civil War and the rising menace of Fascism in Europe, their enduring friendship is a constant reference point in both their lives. Complex passions draw each of the two girls in turn into the drama and grandeur of aristocratic Europe. From the carefree glamour of London high society to the devastation of the battlefields in Spain, Casilda, Joscelin and their families are tragically linked by passion and bloodshed.

'A magnificent international saga'
– *The Bookseller*

Claire Lorrimer

Ortolans

Ortolans – a magnificent house, which held a mysterious grip on those who lived in it, hides a secret the Calverley family did not discover for four hundred years.

Three passionate, remarkable women were to play vital roles during Ortolans' long, violent history. First there was Eleanor, forced into an unhappy marriage to a ruthless adventurer plotting to take over the house. Then hotheaded Sophia, prepared to risk everything to keep the house and finally Emma, the modern woman who wanted it all: the career; the man and the house. It seemed that all would be lost, unless Ortolans finally gave up its incredible secret...

The Silver Link

Until her father died, Adela Carstairs had lived in a secure and loving home. Her happiness was shattered when her mother remarries a cruel, hard-drinking man. With her younger brother and sister, Adela is forced to flee his drunken rages and they escape to London where they seek refuge in the squalor of the back streets. Addie's desperate hope is that her childhood companions, the Mallory twins, will find and rescue them. When all three find themselves caught up in the danger and terror of revolutionary France, the twins prove invaluable. It is then that the link between the twins – and Addie's growing love for one of them – is truly put to the test.

Claire Lorrimer

The Spinning Wheel

Harry, the illegitimate child of a young aristocrat and the daughter of his tutor is fostered by the Pritchetts, a gardener and his wife. Harry grows up in idyllic surroundings with Alice, his foster-sister, sometimes going up to the adjoining big house to play with the beautiful but spoilt Madeline. Though secure at the Pritchetts', nothing can prepare Harry for the revelation of his father's true identity. When the truth finally does emerge, Harry finds he cannot forget the care of those who had brought him up – especially Alice with her deep and enduring love.

A Voice in the Dark

Laura Howard, a young English nurse on holiday in Italy, helps the Contessa dell'Alba return to her home after an illness. Laura is befriended by the family and feels herself drawn to Domenico, the Contessa's blind son. To her horror, she suddenly realises that his life is in danger. Enmeshed in a web of intrigue and confusion, unable to find the source of the threats, Laura despairs of her inability to convince the family that they are in mortal danger. Finally aware of her love for Domenico, she tries desperately to uncover the mystery but she soon finds out that her own life is in danger too...

'Compelling story of love and intrigue'
– *The Bookseller*

CLAIRE LORRIMER

THE WILDERLING

Although born into the British aristocracy, the Honourable Sophia Lucienne Rochford was raised in obscurity first in a French convent and then a Parisian brothel. At sixteen, she is restored to her rightful place as the daughter of the Rochford family, but a devastating betrayal by her father fires her determination to seek wealth and independence at any cost. Denying the existence of love, Lucy makes many tragic mistakes in her attempts to achieve her desires. Earthy, cruel and beautifully told, this is the gripping sequel to *The Chatelaine*.

'A memorable heroine; enthralling and compelling love story of Edwardian England and the First World War'
– *Romantic Times*

OTHER TITLES BY CLAIRE LORRIMER AVAILABLE DIRECT FROM HOUSE OF STRATUS

Quantity		£	$(US)	$(CAN)	€
☐	CHANTAL	6.99	12.95	19.95	13.50
☐	THE CHATELAINE	6.99	12.95	19.95	13.50
☐	FOOL'S CURTAIN	6.99	12.95	19.95	13.50
☐	FROST IN THE SUN	6.99	12.95	19.95	13.50
☐	LAST YEAR'S NIGHTINGALE	6.99	12.95	19.95	13.50
☐	MAVREEN	6.99	12.95	19.95	13.50
☐	ORTOLANS	6.99	12.95	19.95	13.50
☐	RELENTLESS STORM	6.99	12.95	19.95	13.50
☐	THE SHADOW FALLS	6.99	12.95	19.95	13.50
☐	THE SILVER LINK	6.99	12.95	19.95	13.50
☐	THE SPINNING WHEEL	6.99	12.95	19.95	13.50
☐	TAMARISK	6.99	12.95	19.95	13.50
☐	A VOICE IN THE DARK	6.99	12.95	19.95	13.50
☐	THE WILDERLING	6.99	12.95	19.95	13.50

ALL HOUSE OF STRATUS BOOKS ARE AVAILABLE FROM GOOD BOOKSHOPS OR DIRECT FROM THE PUBLISHER:

Internet: **www.houseofstratus.com** including synopses and features.

Email: **sales@houseofstratus.com**
info@houseofstratus.com
(please quote author, title and credit card details.)

Tel: **Order Line**
0800 169 1780 (UK)
800 724 1100 (USA)
International
+44 (0) 1845 527700 (UK)
+01 845 463 1100 (USA)

Fax: **+44 (0) 1845 527711 (UK)**
+01 845 463 0018 (USA)
(please quote author, title and credit card details.)

Send to: **House of Stratus Sales Department**
Thirsk Industrial Park
York Road, Thirsk
North Yorkshire, YO7 3BX
UK

House of Stratus Inc.
2 Neptune Road
Poughkeepsie
NY 12601
USA

PAYMENT

Please tick currency you wish to use:

☐ £ (Sterling) ☐ $ (US) ☐ $ (CAN) ☐ € (Euros)

Allow for shipping costs charged per order plus an amount per book as set out in the tables below:

CURRENCY/DESTINATION

	£(Sterling)	$(US)	$(CAN)	€(Euros)
Cost per order				
UK	1.50	2.25	3.50	2.50
Europe	3.00	4.50	6.75	5.00
North America	3.00	3.50	5.25	5.00
Rest of World	3.00	4.50	6.75	5.00
Additional cost per book				
UK	0.50	0.75	1.15	0.85
Europe	1.00	1.50	2.25	1.70
North America	1.00	1.00	1.50	1.70
Rest of World	1.50	2.25	3.50	3.00

PLEASE SEND CHEQUE OR INTERNATIONAL MONEY ORDER
payable to: HOUSE OF STRATUS LTD or HOUSE OF STRATUS INC. or card payment as indicated

STERLING EXAMPLE

Cost of book(s): .... Example: 3 x books at £6.99 each: £20.97

Cost of order: .... Example: £1.50 (Delivery to UK address)

Additional cost per book: .... Example: 3 x £0.50: £1.50

Order total including shipping: .... Example: £23.97

VISA, MASTERCARD, SWITCH, AMEX:

☐☐☐☐☐☐☐☐☐☐☐☐☐☐☐☐☐☐☐☐

Issue number (Switch only):

☐☐☐

Start Date: ☐☐/☐☐

Expiry Date: ☐☐/☐☐

Signature: ______________________________

NAME: ______________________________

ADDRESS: ______________________________

COUNTRY: ______________________________

ZIP/POSTCODE: ______________________________

Please allow 28 days for delivery. Despatch normally within 48 hours.

Prices subject to change without notice.
Please tick box if you do not wish to receive any additional information. ☐

House of Stratus publishes many other titles in this genre; please check our website (**www.houseofstratus.com**) for more details.